Dr. Jekyll & Mr. Hyde

Retold by John Grant
With introduction and notes by Anthony Marks

Illustrations by
Ron Tiner and Harvey Parker

First published in 2002 by Usborne Publishing Ltd,
Usborne House, 83-85 Saffron Hill, London
EC1N 8RT, England.
www.usborne.com

A catalogue record for this title is available from
the British Library

UK ISBN 07460 51972

First published in America 2004
American ISBN 07945 02385

Printed in Great Britain

Edited by Felicity Brooks & Anthony Marks
Designed by Brian Voakes
Series editors: Jane Chisholm & Rosie Dickins
Series designer: Mary Cartwright
Cover design by Amanda Gulliver
Cover image by Harvey Parker

CONTENTS

About Dr. Jekyll and Mr. Hyde

The strange, thrilling story in this book is a shortened version of *The Strange Case of Dr. Jekyll and Mr. Hyde*, by Scottish novelist Robert Louis Stevenson. Stevenson was born in Scotland in 1850. He trained as a lawyer, but in 1873 he went to France to recover from a lung infection and it was then that his career as an author began. By the end of the decade he had written two travel books, including *Travels with a Donkey in the Cévennes* (1879), and published many articles and stories in magazines. Stevenson lived in several countries during his life, partly because he believed the cold, damp Scottish climate was bad for his health, and partly because he was adventurous and wanted to see the world. Apart from France, he spent time in the USA, Switzerland and Samoa, where he died in 1894. *Dr. Jekyll and Mr. Hyde (*1886), the book that brought Stevenson widespread popularity, was written while he was living in England. His other famous novels include *Treasure Island* (1883), *Prince Otto* (1885) and *Kidnapped* (1886).

Dr. Jekyll and Mr. Hyde charts the terrifying downfall of Henry Jekyll, a society doctor who invents a potion that alters his character. While under the influence of this drug, Jekyll becomes Edward Hyde, a man without any sense of good or evil who, acting like a wild animal, commits hideous crimes. Gradually Jekyll loses control over his evil counterpart, with dreadful consequences. This novel, like others by Stevenson, contains elements of mystery and suspense. However, compared to adventure stories such as *Treasure Island*, the ideas it explores are very different.

Much of *Dr. Jekyll and Mr. Hyde* is about hiding and concealing. Many people think Stevenson was commenting on Victorian society, pointing out that while rich and influential people pretended to be good, their lives often hid evil secrets. Some say he was also talking about hidden aspects of his own character. The story is set in Victorian London, where rich and poor, and good and evil, lived side by side. While London was one of the richest and most beautiful cities in Europe, it contained some of the poorest people, living in terrible conditions. The book tells us that cities, like people, can hide squalid, unpleasant parts behind impressive, elegant facades. It describes how the exteriors of buildings look different from their interiors, or the fronts look different from the backs. Additionally, many of the characters conceal things from each other. Jekyll hides his experiments from friends and colleagues (even Hyde's name is a pun); Richard Enfield at first hides Jekyll's identity from Utterson; and Utterson hides information from the police. The way the story is written uses concealment, too – many facts are hidden in scribbled notes, messages and letters, or letters within letters. Stevenson even hides some of the basic elements of a standard plot; for instance, the book has no real hero, and though there is an end to the story there is no real conclusion.

The 19th century was a period of great scientific development and many novels from the time, including *Dr. Jekyll and Mr. Hyde,* have science and the pursuit of knowledge as themes. Jekyll begins his experiments with good intentions. But he later admits to his friend, Hastie Lanyon, that he was driven to conduct more daring experiments by vanity, because he wanted the medical world to hail him as a great scientist. As his work progresses, he becomes addicted to the evil world of Mr. Hyde, finding it harder to shake him off, until in the end his quest for knowledge destroys him. In this way, Stevenson asks who is more wicked: the scientist's creation, with little sense of good and bad; or the scientist himself, who knows his experiments are wrong but prolongs them for personal gain. These problems still concern us today, which may well be why *Dr. Jekyll and Mr. Hyde* remains one of the most popular novels ever written.

Inside the Cabinet

If houses are faces, the house you're standing in front of is the stony face of a stern teacher who knows that the children are up to something but doesn't know exactly what. Yet behind this face is a household that is happy enough. The house is owned by a doctor, originally from somewhere on the Scottish borders. Dr. Jekyll came here to London some decades ago, after graduating from university. His household is managed by a staunch, rather silent man, the butler Poole, and by a cook and a handful of young servants. They regard him as a good, kind and considerate master and are loyal to him.

Coming around the side of the house you find a yard, partly covered in paving stones and partly cultivated as a vegetable garden. On the far side of the yard is an outhouse, built by the place's previous owner – a surgeon – as his dissecting room, a surgical theatre in which he used to give practical anatomy lessons to students. Nowadays this little building is called the Cabinet, and Dr. Jekyll often performs his experiments there.

He is doing so tonight. The rest of his household has gone to bed, but a light still burns in the window of the Cabinet. Wiping the greasy fog off the glass with the back of your hand, you can peer through the window to see Dr. Jekyll at work. He is leaning forward intently over his laboratory bench. A lock of his silvery-grey hair, which he wears rather long, has flopped down across his forehead, and he impatiently flicks it away with a toss of his head. In one hand he holds a glass beaker half-filled with a clear, blood-red liquid. In the other is a fold of paper containing a small heap of white powder. Sucking his lower lip in concentration, he slowly and carefully taps a little of the powder into the liquid. For a moment the surface of the liquid froths. As he gently shakes the beaker, the liquid changes, becoming a steely blue.

Cautiously he adds some more of the powder. And then some more. When at last all the powder has been used up, the potion in the beaker is dirty brown like a puddle.

He looks around him furtively, as if he senses you watching him through the window, and then for the first time in many minutes he dares to let out a deep breath. He twirls the beaker a few more times, and stands up. He climbs the few stairs that lead to the door of the Cabinet's smaller room. You can no longer see him, but through the open door you can watch the flickering candlelight make dancing shadows on the bare wall of the smaller room.

For a moment there is nothing else to see. Then a roar of anguish and despair – a roar you will never be able to forget – splits the silence of the deserted yard. There is a loud crash and the sound of breaking glass.

After a short while, a figure appears in the doorway at the top of the stairs – a small man, clutching at the door frame for support. He is younger than Dr. Jekyll, but he is wearing the doctor's clothes, which are several sizes too large for him; this should look comical, but it doesn't. The man's face, although not ugly, has a look of such malignance and cruelty that the breath catches in your throat. Although the fingers that hold onto the door frame are undoubtedly human, they make you think of a predatory bird's powerful claws.

Now strength is coming into the man, so he can push himself away from the door and stand upright. You can see the ferocious physical power coiled into the slight figure. It looks as if he is ready at any instant to explode into swift violence.

He raises that hateful face and you see his eyes, which are the worst of all. They are black and hard, and they seem to you like the openings to dark and perilous corridors.

And they are looking straight at you.

A Devil on our Streets

It had been a good dinner party.

Richard Enfield came to the corner of the street and leaned against the wall. Three o'clock in the morning and London was bitterly cold and seemingly deserted. Since leaving the Connaughts' house on the other side of the river he had seen only two other people, and once a hackney carriage had clopped by in the distance. For a moment, leaning there, he wished that he had hailed just such a carriage to take him home, but then he straightened his shoulders. He had decided that the cold night air was just what he needed to flush the effects of the evening's wine out of his brain, and indeed it had succeeded. The fog that had hung over the city earlier, making the air feel like thin, clammy glue, had lifted. The night was crisp and clear.

Pushing himself away from the wall, he turned the corner and came into a street that was unfamiliar to him. At least... The sign over a shop window jogged his memory. This was Mitre Street, and he knew it well enough in the daytime, when the gaudy contents of cheap shops spilled out onto the pavement and throngs of people in coarse, knitted clothing shouted and laughed and haggled. At night, when only the hiss of the gaslights and the echoes of his own footsteps were in the air, it seemed a different place altogether.

But then, when he was halfway down Mitre Street, he heard another sound – a voice.

"And mind you tell Dr. Strachan how much pain your Mam's in," said a man from a sidestreet off to the left. "Tell him to come quick, Mabel!"

"Yes, Da," said a child's voice, sounding resigned. Pausing, Richard could hear the girl's footsteps, and now he could see her in the distance, running towards him in the gaslight, her long nightdress tangling between her legs so that she kept half-tripping. He guessed she must be six or seven years old – very young to be out so late on a night as cold as this. He wondered if he ought to offer to help, to go with her to Dr. Strachan's house, wherever that might be.

Before he could decide, he heard another set of footsteps. Coming up Mitre Street at a fast walk was a small man dressed, like Richard himself, in a top hat, a dark tailcoat, a starched white shirt and a bow tie. Perhaps it was Dr. Strachan, already alerted to the crisis. Richard grinned. He might not have been sober at the start of his long walk home, but certainly he must look tidier than this gentleman. The bow tie had come almost undone, and there was a dark smudge of something on his shirt.

Richard twirled his cane and started to stroll onwards, but something made him look round to see what happened next. The child and the scruffy little man arrived at the corner at the same moment. The child, startled by the sudden encounter, made a move to dodge aside, but the man kept walking at that same rapid, determined pace; kept walking and trampled the girl underfoot.

Richard swore, and clenched his fist on his cane. "What the... ?"

The child's head hit the pavement with a loud *crack*. For an instant Richard thought she must have fractured her skull, but then she began to cry and then scream in pain and shock.

"Come back here, you swine!" yelled Richard.

The man paid him no attention, but continued to march ahead as if he were totally ignorant of what he had done to the child.

"Hey! You!" Gathering his coat tails around him and wielding his cane like a club, Richard began to chase him. He ran across the road, paused beside the screaming child to make sure she was not seriously injured, then sprinted after the swiftly receding man.

He caught up with him at the open mouth of a little side court, into which the small man was just turning. Dropping his own cane, Richard lunged forward and grabbed the other man by the collar.

"Hey! What the devil do you mean by... ?"

"Take your hands off me!"

It was a threatening snarl, and Richard almost obeyed. But then he tightened his grip. "No, sir!" he snapped. "You have something to account for before I let you go!"

His captive twisted around to look him in the eyes. Richard flinched. Then the man's fearful gaze dropped to look back along the street, where someone, presumably the girl's father, was cradling her in his arms, trying to calm her. Candlelight was beginning to appear in the windows on either side.

"A street child," sneered the man in Richard's grasp. "It is a matter of no consequence."

"Why, you..." Richard began, but then he saved his breath for the task of dragging the little man back to the scene of the incident. After struggling once or twice his captive came along easily enough, but Richard didn't loosen his hold.

Now there were several other people gathered around the child. "Mabel, Mabel," said the man holding her across his knees, her head clasped to his chest. "Hush your noise, Mabel, and tell your old Da what happened."

She gulped, drew breath and began to scream again when she saw the man standing beside Richard.

"I saw," said Richard. "This... this *gentleman*" – he filled his voice with sarcasm – "this devil on our

streets, this foul *creature* knocked your daughter to the ground and trampled her. He should be whipped. In fact, I've a good mind to... "

"Make room," said a voice from the far side of the little crowd.

Mabel's father, who had been fixing the scruffy man with a look of pure hatred, hesitantly turned his gaze away. "Dr. Strachan," he said quietly. "God must have sent you to where you are needed."

Strachan spared Richard and his prisoner hardly a glance but dropped down on one knee beside Mabel and her father. His presence seemed to calm the girl, because her screaming stuttered to a reluctant halt. He ran his fingers rapidly over Mabel's limbs, pressing gently here and there, then repeated the process with her chest and back. Finally he probed carefully beneath her hair.

"She'll have a lump the size of a goose egg on her head tomorrow, Sam," he said at last, "and she may have a greenstick fracture of her left forearm, but she'll live. I'll bandage up her arm and give her something to help her sleep tonight. Time enough in the morning to put her in splints."

"Dr. Strachan," said Mabel's father, "God bless you. But you know I have no money to..."

Strachan waved his hand impatiently. "Nonsense, Sam. You're an honest man, and I know you'll pay me when and if you can. And, even if you can't, your friendship is reward enough for me."

Richard had remained silent for several minutes, merely holding on to his captive's collar and trying not to look at the man's face. There was something terrifying about it that froze the blood. Now he intervened.

"Friendship doesn't fill many stomachs," he said. "Someone should settle your bill."

"Who might you be?" said Strachan sharply.

"I witnessed everything," Richard said, and quickly described what he'd seen.

"So I say," he concluded, "that either we can call a police constable and have this scoundrel thrown in prison for the night, or we can ask the rogue to pay young Mabel here sufficient compensation for her pain, with enough left over to settle all that Sam might owe you, Dr. Strachan. I'd say one hundred pounds should suffice."

"Or we could string him up from the nearest lamp post," muttered someone.

Strachan looked at the little man, his lip curling back with obvious distaste. "That may be a grand amount for Sam here," he said, "but the man who can afford those shoes would hardly notice it. A hundred pounds would scarcely seem enough... "

"I'll give you a hundred," said the small man unexpectedly, "if only you'll persuade this wretched thug to let go of my collar."

Strachan looked startled. "Do you mean that?"

"I said it, didn't I?"

"What's your name?" said Strachan, rising to his feet. "I seem to have seen you somewhere before." His look had turned to one of loathing.

"Well, I assure you that I've never laid eyes on *you*, sir!" said the small man. "Now, will you accept my offer or won't you? Speak, man, before I change my mind."

"There's always the lamp post," said Richard softly.

The little man stiffened, then relaxed. "Come with me to my house and I'll give you the money."

"I'll come too," said Richard flatly.

"What is your name?" hissed Strachan again to the little man.

"Hyde. My name is Hyde, as if it were any concern of yours, you backstreet sawbones."

Richard unobtrusively edged his body between the two men. "Your wife," he said to Sam. "You sent young Mabel to fetch Dr. Strachan for your wife."

Strachan eased his stance and turned away. "Sam," he said, "I'd better go and see Alice, if she's ill. Then I'll follow after you to this creature's lair."

"Mitre Court," said Hyde, suddenly seeming eager that the doctor should not abandon him. Richard was a tall man, and Mabel's father even taller. "Number Two, Mitre Court."

"I'll follow you," Strachan confirmed, and moved briskly away.

"One hundred pounds," said Hyde, fumbling with the key. Somehow, throughout the entire proceedings, he had managed to keep hold of his walking cane, which Richard noticed for the first time. The handle was silver, and cast in the form of a devil's head. "You gentlemen will wait here."

Richard looked around him. Mitre Court was set back a little from the street. It was covered with litter and smelled of decay. Light trickled unwillingly in from the gas lamps along Mitre Street. There were too many dark shadows for his liking. He shivered, not entirely because of the cold.

"What guarantee do we have that you won't dart out some back entrance?" he said.

"You have my word," Hyde said.

Richard snorted derisively.

"This place has no other street entrance," said Sam, his voice hoarse. Richard could see he was controlling his rage with difficulty. "There's no other way out."

Hyde looked at him gratefully as the door opened at last. "I'll be no more than a minute," he said, and disappeared inside.

To Richard's surprise, Hyde was as good as his word and returned to the door after a short while.

"I've only ten pounds in cash," he said, counting the sovereigns into Sam's outstretched hand. "You will have to accept a cheque for the remainder."

He produced the cheque with a flourish. Sam looked blank, and then began to growl quietly with disapproval.

"Our friend here does not patronize banks," said Richard. "He has no way to cash your cheque."

"Then you may cash it for him," said Hyde irritably, clearly wanting to shut the door on them. "I have made it payable to 'Bearer'." He pushed the piece of paper into Richard's hands.

Richard looked at it. The cheque seemed genuine enough. But then he saw the signature, *Henry Jekyll*, written in a large, elegant script. It was hard to imagine the claw-like, ever-twitching fingers of Hyde writing such a signature.

"Who's this Jekyll?" he said.

"A friend of mine. He was inside, and gave me the cheque to help me out of... my little difficulty."

"Where is he? Let us see him," said Richard.

"I'm afraid that would be... inconvenient." A sudden look of worry crossed Hyde's strangely repellent face.

"Then how do we know this cheque is worth the paper it's written on?"

"Because... because I will stay with you until the morning, when we can take it to my bank." The words were spoken impulsively, in a single blurt.

"And I will stay too," said Strachan, appearing out of the gloom.

"It is barely a mile to my rooms," said Richard, "and I have several bottles of fine port which I would willingly share with you."

"Then consider the matter settled," said the doctor, rubbing his hands together.

Sam looked uneasy. Strachan did his best to reassure him that his wife and daughter were in no immediate danger, but the man was obviously not entirely convinced. Politely declining Richard's offer of port, he arranged to meet them outside the bank the following morning and then strode off briskly in the direction of his home.

Some months later, Richard was out taking a Sunday walk with his cousin, Gabriel Utterson, when they happened to find themselves in Mitre Street. Pausing opposite Mitre Court, Richard was suddenly reminded of the strange events of that night, and he told his elderly cousin about the loathsome little man who had trampled down the child. He was careful not to mention Henry Jekyll, for in the meantime he'd heard that Jekyll was a highly respected doctor as well as a tireless worker for charity.

21

"To be sure," he concluded, "I counted my spoons in the morning, even though Strachan and I had taken turns through the night to stay awake watching the foul creature."

"And the cheque?" said Utterson. He was a lawyer and widely admired for his honesty and discretion. He had a craggy, severe-looking face and rarely smiled, though his eyes often twinkled with secret mirth or compassion. There was no twinkle in them now. His face was a mask of worry and bewilderment. "The cheque with another man's name on it — was it valid?"

"It was fine," said Richard. "Even though we had Hyde with us, I expected the bank to reject it out of hand as a forgery, but they accepted it immediately. When I pressed the cashier he said that he had met Hyde before; that this was not the first time the rogue had drawn money on that man's account."

Utterson drew a deep sigh. "What was the name on the cheque?" he said.

"The name is that of a good man," said Richard. "I have no wish to see that name tarnished. My conclusion is that the poor fellow is being blackmailed by this Hyde for some minor sin he committed in his youth. Whatever it might have been, it has surely been more than made up for by his good deeds since."

Utterson sighed again. "I fear," he said, "that I already know the name. I was only asking you to confirm the worst. This is sad news you have told me, Richard my friend. Very sad news indeed." He looked away, his eyes focused on something infinitely far away. "Sad news," he repeated under his breath.

"What's the matter?" said Richard. "Is he a friend of yours?"

"A friend and a client," replied Utterson. "I can't tell you any more than that. As a client he's entitled to my confidentiality."

Richard nodded. "Then why are you so certain that you... ?"

"I know that door," said Utterson brusquely.

"Your friend Sam was wrong when he said that there was no other street entrance. There is. Number Two Mitre Court is the outbuilding to another, greater house. The owner of that... No, I've said too much already."

"I don't want to pry," said Richard, "but is there any way we could help Jek... help your friend escape the clutches of this vile blackmailer? It is blackmail, I assume."

"No," said Utterson bleakly. "There's nothing you can do, and perhaps precious little that I can."

"But it's *blackmail!*" Richard exclaimed.

Utterson looked at him with eyes that were as cold and despairing as an arctic wind.

"Blackmail," he said. "It might be. Or it could be something far worse..."

The Lawyer and the Will

Shortly after the discussion in Mitre Street, Gabriel Utterson made some excuse to cut the walk short. Leaving Richard on a street corner looking out for a cab, he set off at a rapid pace for his own home. The sunny sky of earlier in the day had disappeared behind a thick carpet of grey cloud, and a brisk, cold wind was blowing through the streets. But this was not the reason why Utterson gripped his coat firmly around him. The chill he was trying to shield himself from was the chill of his own fears.

However, when he reached home the haste melted from his movements. He called out to his manservant, Molyneaux, that he had returned, then carefully arranged his coat and hat on the stand in the hall. There was a fire crackling in the upstairs drawing room, and the lawyer settled himself on a leather-covered chair in front of it, leaning forwards with his hands out towards the flames.

Several minutes passed, and Utterson eased slowly further and further back in the chair, his feet stretched out in front of him. Anyone looking at him would have thought that his gaze was fixed on the fireplace, but he saw nothing of it. His mind was focused on the scene in his office downstairs, when he had last seen his old friend Dr. Henry Jekyll.

Molyneaux glided in silently with a glass of dry sherry on a silver tray, and placed it on a little table by the arm of his master's chair.

Utterson muttered some acknowledgment, then raised the glass to his lips and drained it in a couple of gulps, barely conscious of what he was doing.

Molyneaux, seeing his master's mood, retreated from the room, then reappeared a few moments later with the decanter.

"Dinner will be served in fifteen minutes," said the servant, as if addressing the room in general. Again, Utterson mumbled something incomprehensible.

He ate dinner without tasting anything, his attention still far away, and after the meal took a glass of wine and a candle and went slowly down the stairs to the room that he used as an office. Molyneaux exchanged a glance with Annie, the maid. Always on a Sunday evening their master would sit in front of the drawing room fire reading a book until the clock chimed midnight. But not tonight. Something must have disturbed him greatly.

Not for the first time, Utterson thought that the flickering candlelight made his office feel haunted. The tall filing cabinet near the window seemed to be a plump, old lady leaning forward trying to hear any whisper that he might make. The shadows beneath the room's smaller desk, the one that was used during the day by his occasional clerk, Mr. Guest, appeared to be filled with dancing shapes, as if tonight were the night when the King of the Rats was holding his ghostly ball. The eyes in the oil portrait on the wall seemed alive, watching Utterson frostily.

The elderly lawyer seized the portrait by its imposing frame and lifted it clear of its hook. Set into the wall behind was a safe. Its face was dusty, but the dials of its combination lock shone brightly from frequent use. Putting the candlestick down on the larger of the two desks, Utterson reached up wearily to turn the dials.

A minute later he was seated at his desk, staring at the document he had pulled from the dark recesses of the safe. It had been folded in four, and at first he seemed reluctant to open it out. But at last he did so, and in the candle's uncertain yellow light he began to read it.

The document was a will; the will of Dr. Henry Jekyll. Utterson had read it several times before and knew its contents well; as he read it now his lips moved slightly, as if he were reciting a litany under his breath.

Jekyll had come to him several months before to discuss the making of this will. The lawyer had listened to him intently and then, when the doctor had finished explaining what he wanted to do, had thrown up his hands and begun to protest loudly.

"But this is nonsense, old friend!" Utterson had exclaimed. "Who is this man Hyde? I've known you for more years than I care to remember, Henry, and I've never heard you even mention his name. Does he have some sort of hold over you?"

But Jekyll had sat quietly on the edge of his chair, his hands folded primly in his lap. "My relationship to Edward Hyde is no concern of yours," he had said rather coldly. "You are my lawyer, Gabriel, not my confessor."

"But I'm also your friend, Henry. If you're in trouble, old man..."

"There is nothing more I wish to add," said Jekyll, closing the subject. "Will you make up my new will for me, Gabriel, or must I take my business to another lawyer after all these years?"

Utterson had breathed a heavy sigh.

"No, Henry. There's no need to find another lawyer. I'll hold your will for you, as I've always done.

But I can't bring myself to draw up this new will for you – that's something you'll have to do yourself."

So, with Utterson's help on the formal, legalistic wording, Jekyll had written out his new will. In it he left everything to his "friend and benefactor Edward Hyde". If this had been all, the lawyer would not have objected so strenuously. But there was an extra clause: Hyde was also to inherit everything Jekyll owned should the doctor "disappear or be absent without explanation for any period exceeding three months." This was what had offended Gabriel Utterson. To his sober and orderly mind, people in adventure stories might disappear mysteriously, but not well-established doctors with respectable positions in society. Besides, Utterson knew nothing at all about Hyde: if the man was a villain and knew the generous – the *over*-generous – provisions of the will, might he not be tempted to get rid of Jekyll? After the doctor's disappearance for three months, Hyde would be a rich man, and could flee abroad with the profits from his crime.

Now Utterson shuddered. Over the past few months, whenever he had worried about Jekyll's will, he'd been able to tell himself that he was just being a silly old fool, fretting over nothing: for all he had known Edward Hyde might have been a saint. But today, thanks to his conversation in the street with Richard, he knew otherwise. Some of the words Richard had used came back to him. Hyde had a "fearful gaze". There was something about the man's face that "froze the blood". And Richard said that he had small, hard, evil eyes...

Utterson shuddered again. The candle had burned low while he'd been lost in thought, and the flame was guttering. He picked up the will, handling it as if it were somehow unclean. "Henry must have sunk very low indeed to find himself in the clutches of such a villain," he muttered to himself as he slid the will back into its stiff, cardboard envelope. "I fear he must have done something awful. If it were only some minor indiscretion, surely he'd have braved the shame of exposure to rid himself of this parasite Hyde. No, it must be a *terrible* secret if he's so concerned to conceal it."

Molyneaux appeared in the hall just as Utterson was locking the door of his office behind him.

"What time is it, Molyneaux?"

"It is a quarter to ten," said the servant.

"A bit late," said Utterson, half to himself. "But Lanyon has never been one for an early night." More loudly, he said: "I'm going out to visit Dr. Lanyon. Bring my coat and stick. I may not be back before midnight, so there's no need to wait up for me."

Meanwhile, somewhere half-across London, in the middle of a network of narrow alleyways where the glow of the gas lamps seems to fight a losing battle against the darkness of human misery, a small man flits from shadow to shadow. It is Edward Hyde.

In one hand he carries a bottle, in the other a walking cane with a most distinctive silver handle, shaped in the form of a devil's head. Apart from the occasional glint of light on glass or silver, or on the teeth that show whitely between drawn-back lips, the small figure could be a shadow himself.

On the corner of Garter Lane and Langford Mews is a pub, the Groat and Sixpence. Light spills from its grimy windows; drunken shouting pours from its door. Inside, someone is playing loudly and badly on a cracked accordion while other voices are raised in discordant song. There is the sound of glass breaking. Hyde pauses at the door, enjoying the noise.

There is little pleasure to be found in this part of London, and what is available is normally paid for the next morning in the form of aching heads and broken limbs. The noise is the sound of people destroying their own lives. He likes it.

Dropping his bottle on the pavement, he throws open the door and steps into the thick, smelly air of the pub. Tobacco smoke greys the light of the lamps. The pungent stench of cheap gin is everywhere. More than one of the customers is stretched out on the floor, snoring, pockets presumably already ransacked. In the corner two old men – forty is an age that passes for old in these parts – are arm-wrestling, watched by a woman in scarlet lipstick and a too-broad smile.

The pub becomes briefly quiet as the new arrival picks his way to the bar.

"Champagne," says Hyde.

The landlord, a huge man with tattoos up both arms, gives a mirthless snort of laughter. "We don't

serve that kind of drink here," he says firmly. "I think you've wandered from your path, guv'nor. This is no place for a fine gentleman like you."

Hyde giggles. It is a strange, high sound that picks at the mind as if trying to uncover things that are best left covered. This time, when the racket of the pub grows quiet, it stays that way. Two or three hands stray towards hidden knives.

"In that case I'll have whatever wine you sell," insists Hyde.

The landlord glares at him, then abruptly glances away, looking oddly frightened.

"I told you before," he says in a low voice. "This isn't the place for the likes of you."

Hyde's cane comes whistling down to hammer the sticky wooden surface of the bar. Further along, a glass left perched on the bar's edge teeters and falls with a crash to the floor. The sharp sound fades away into complete silence.

"Then tell me what drink you do have that a gentleman might sample," snarls Hyde.

"We have gin," says the landlord nervously. "And ale. And cider. Nothing else." Clearly he feels that he should throw this stranger out into the street, and can't understand why he's not doing so.

"Gin, then!" says Hyde. "A bottle of it! But if you're forcing a gentleman to drink such muck you're surely not expecting him to pay for it. Are you?"

"No one drinks in the Groat and Sixpence that doesn't pay their way," says the landlord stolidly, mustering his resentment.

"And is that something you wish to argue about?" says Hyde quietly, leaning forward over the bar, his eyes steely.

The landlord holds his stare for a long moment, but then his gaze falters once more.

"No," he mumbles. "No. I don't want to argue with you."

When Utterson reached Hastie Lanyon's home in Cavendish Square, the doctor was indeed still up. Although he was visibly surprised to see Utterson this late at night, and glanced curiously at the lawyer's wind-blown clothing and perspiring face, he welcomed his old friend. Once they were settled in front of the fire, he looked over the top of his spectacles.

"It's been more than a year since last I saw you," he said.

"Old friends have a habit of not seeing each other for long stretches at a time," said Utterson. "And it's about old friends that I've come to see you, Hastie."

Lanyon continued to regard him steadily over his gold-rimmed glasses.

"It's about Jekyll," Utterson began.

"Jekyll!" The elderly doctor leaped to his feet and paced across the carpet to the window. There was nothing visible outside except the movement of skeletal trees against the lamplight. "The man's a fool!"

"Come now, old chap..."

"A fool, I tell you!" Lanyon turned from the window and stared earnestly at Utterson. "I used to count him as one of my closest friends, certainly my closest in the medical profession, yet he began to talk such drivel that I felt I had to estrange myself from him before I became associated with his lunatic ideas. And it wasn't just the opinions of my colleagues I was worried about, let me tell you. The unscientific, hare-brained theories he insisted on spouting were an insult to my intelligence! To our friendship! I told him more than once to keep his claptrap to himself, but he persisted. I had little choice but to stop seeing him! I run into him from time to time, of course. As doctors we occasionally find ourselves in the same company. But I can tell you, dear chap, that nowadays I take great care to make sure that my relationship with Henry Jekyll consists of no more than that!"

Utterson nodded, as if in sympathy. The thin old doctor's face was beginning to flush and threatened to become purple. The lawyer sensed that, if he defended Jekyll too well, he would find himself shown out to the street.

"I'm sorry to hear that," he murmured.

His soft words seemed to soothe Lanyon, for after a few more agitated paces the doctor sat down once more in the chair opposite Utterson. They talked of other matters for a while, as old acquaintances do.

At last the conversation turned back to Jekyll. Speaking carefully, not wanting to spark off another outburst, Utterson said: "There's a friend of his you may have come across – a fellow called Hyde. Do you know anything about him?"

"Hyde?" repeated Lanyon, taking off his spectacles and toying with them. "No, I can't say the name means anything to me. It's a common enough name, of course, but... No, I don't remember Jekyll ever saying anything about a Hyde. Why do you ask?"

"It's nothing important," said Utterson casually. He switched the subject swiftly. "Do you ever hear from old MacFinnon?"

It was well past midnight when he left the doctor's house. He had learned very little from Lanyon, but the old man's outburst about Jekyll had puzzled him and, if anything, made him even more uneasy than before. Crazy scientific theories? Even the phrase was enough to disconcert the lawyer, whose opinion of progress was that it had been an entirely undesirable invention.

When he finally reached home, the house was cold and dark. The servants had gone to bed. Utterson was grumpy because they had done so, and the knowledge that he himself had told them not to wait up only made him grumpier. He muttered crossly to himself as, candle in hand, he made his way up the long, curving staircase to his bedroom.

That night, sleep proved to be elusive. His bed seemed much lumpier than usual; his pillow might as well have been a block of wood for all the comfort it gave him, and the linen pillowcase seemed damp. He pulled the covers up over his head as the bell on the clock tower of St. Gregory's rang out for two o'clock.

He fell into a state halfway between sleeping and wakefulness. He knew that he was in his bed, but at the same time he seemed to be watching brightly-lit scenes that were happening somewhere else in London. Richard's description that afternoon of the little man trampling the girl underfoot came back to him, and he watched the incident play itself out again and again. Now it was as if he were soaring high over London, so that the whole city was laid out below him like a map; and on every corner, as far in the distance as he could see, there was an evil little man stamping a child to the ground.

He turned over, and as he did so the scene changed. Now he seemed to be in the darkened bedroom of a grand house. Just enough moonlight came in through the windows for him to see the form of his old friend, Henry Jekyll, stretched out on the bed. Jekyll appeared to be asleep, or was he... was he dead? Utterson tried to move from his position in the corner to see, but he found himself powerless: he was here only as a spectator, not as an actor in the scene.

Then the door of Jekyll's bedroom was thrown open, and a wedge of light from the passage fell across the floor. Silhouetted in the doorway was a small figure dressed in fine clothes – or clothes that had been fine, for the pocket on one side of the coat was torn, the white shirt was smudged, and the bow tie had been pulled around until it was nearly under the small figure's ear.

Somehow Utterson knew without question that the intruder was Hyde. And he knew Hyde was speaking, barking out instructions to the sleeping Jekyll, even though in his dream he could hear no voice. As Jekyll, moving like a sleepwalker, pulled himself up on the bed and got to his feet, Hyde came closer to the corner where Utterson stood, peering into the shadows as if he suspected that somebody was lurking there. In the dim light Utterson could see a malevolent gleam in the little man's eyes, but nothing more of his face.

And then, much worse, he could see that his vision of Hyde *had* no face.

The old lawyer sat up in bed with a jolt, clutching the blankets around him and staring at the grey dawn light of his bedroom. His mouth was open, but the scream he was about to give died before it had properly formed. In the distance, the bell of St. Gregory's rang, telling the world that it was six o'clock in the morning.

Although Gabriel Utterson still worked as a lawyer, he had allowed his business to run down over the past few years. He had earned enough money over the course of a long career to pick and choose whether he worked or not. Those few clients that still remained were either old friends or had become so. His duties consisted largely of the drawing up of wills or, increasingly frequently these days, the reading of them after the funeral.

As he ate his breakfast that morning, he realized that, unless one or other of his clients died, he had no especially pressing duties to attend to during the next few weeks. Mr. Guest, his clerk, could cope with day-to-day affairs. Utterson was free, if he wanted to, to indulge himself in a bit of detective work.

"Silly games," he mumbled to himself as Annie cleared his plate away. "Childish games. Highly unsuitable for an elderly gentleman like me. But..."

The "but" was enough to take him out onto the street, safely buttoned up in his overcoat, and to turn his steps in the direction of Mitre Street. He had no clear idea of what it was he was planning to do, except that he wanted to track down Hyde. From Richard's description, he knew that this was where the evil little man had trampled down the girl – and as he told himself, "if he can be Mr. Hyde, then I will be Mr. Seek."

He was an odd figure among the hawkers and traders of Mitre Street that first day, but most of the tradespeople were friendly. They soon started calling him "Your Lordship", a nickname he initially found irritating but soon came to accept as something of a compliment.

Accustomed to a cooked three-course lunch, he nevertheless found great satisfaction in making a meal out of apples and cheese from one of the stalls, and to wash it down he bought a bottle of beer, a drink he hadn't had since his student days.

Brushing the cheese crumbs from the front of his coat, he belched quietly and wondered what all his colleagues in the law and his servants would think of him if they could have seen him now.

That first day he was tired when he came home, but happy. The blood seemed to be coursing through his veins. When he went to bed – which was just after ten o'clock, and not around midnight as usual – he slept soundly the whole night through. Without dreaming.

In this way the lawyer passed the next fifteen days. They were a time of happiness for Gabriel Utterson as he began to feel more and more at home in Mitre Street. Gradually he became reluctant to leave at the end of the day, staying there later and later, until Molyneaux and Annie gave up having his dinner ready for him at seven o'clock each evening.

And at last he found his prey.

It was a little after ten o'clock on a frosty evening. For once, miraculously, there was no suspicion of fog in the air. The stallholders had long ago packed up their wares and retreated to their homes for the night. Utterson was just beginning to think that he should do likewise when he heard, clearly in the distance despite the hiss of the streetlamps, the sound of someone taking short and very rapid strides.

It was his man. It had to be. Cocking his head, Utterson listened intently as the footsteps grew closer and closer.

Instinctively he drew back to conceal himself, and clutched his stick more tightly. The footsteps suddenly became louder as the walker rounded the end of the street. Utterson peeped out, his breath steaming in front of him. There was the little man Richard had described. Utterson's dreams had shown him surprisingly accurately. Hyde obviously didn't notice the lawyer, for he kept walking at the same brisk pace, crossing the road and making straight for the door in Mitre Court, pulling a key from his pocket as he went.

Utterson moved without thinking. He reached the little man just as he was turning the key in the lock.

He touched him on the shoulder. "Mr. Hyde, I think?"

Hyde flinched from the touch, but didn't turn. "That's my name," he said. "What do you want? Who are you?"

"An old friend of Henry Jekyll's," said the lawyer. "He must surely have mentioned my name – Gabriel Utterson of Gaunt Street. Let me come in with you to see him."

"Jekyll's not here," said the little man, wriggling his shoulder away. "Go away." He shook his shoulder again, as if he were a dog shaking off water. Then he paused before adding: "And how did you know my name?"

"We have mutual friends," said Utterson, trying to sound casual. "They told me what you looked like."

"Mutual friends?" The little man sounded incredulous. Still he did not turn around. "Who?"

"Well, Henry Jekyll for one."

"Jekyll never spoke to you about me!" snapped Hyde. "You're lying."

Hyde spoke with such certainty that for a moment Utterson was completely flabbergasted. How could Hyde know? But the lawyer continued speaking, anxious not to lose his fish now that he at last had it on the hook.

"Please do one thing for me," he said.

"What?" said Hyde waspishly.

"Turn around, so that I can see your face."

Hyde shrugged and began to obey. For a moment Utterson thought in terror that Hyde would prove as faceless as in those half-waking nightmares. Then, when he was able to look full on the face that was revealed in the gaslight, he almost wished that his premonition had been correct. Those hard, staring, inhumanly wicked eyes were just as he had seen them. The rest of the face seemed unremarkable at first, but immediately afterwards a powerful sense of evil flowed through the lawyer.

He took a nervous step back. "Utterson's the name," he babbled. "Gabriel Utterson... of Gaunt Street. Jekyll's lawyer, as well as his friend. Here, take my business card."

Hyde took the card and looked at it briefly, then tucked it away in his jacket pocket.

"I may have need of you one day. One day soon." The voice was suddenly sinister and calculating.

He knows about the will, thought Utterson. *He knows about it, and he plans to kill Jekyll and...*

"So you had better have my address," continued Hyde. "In case you ever need to find me in a hurry. In case there's an emergency." Utterson's blood chilled at the way Hyde pronounced the word "emergency", deliberately, and with a sort of cloying fondness. "You'll find my lodgings at 43 Staplers' Gate. That is in Soho, off Greek Street. I would give you my address on a prettily engraved business card like your own but, you see, I am a man of only humble means."

He turned back to the door and twisted the key, then added two more words, as if as an afterthought.

"As yet."

And then he was gone, and the door slammed in Utterson's face.

The Door to the Dissecting Room

Poole wound the grandfather clock in the hall, as he always did before going to bed. It was nearly half past ten, and he was tired, yet he didn't feel sleepy. For the past few months, no one in Dr. Jekyll's house was finding it easy to sleep. Not since... not since things had *changed*.

He sighed deeply, the breath sounding like the wind sweeping autumn leaves along the pavement. He was old. He had been old when he had come into Dr. Jekyll's service twenty years ago. By all rights he should have long ago retired, spent his savings on a country cottage and devoted the rest of his life to his garden. But Dr. Jekyll had been insistent that he should stay on. "Good butlers are the very devil to find these days, Poole," he had said, "and there can be no one else like you. Do stay on, there's a good chap. I'd be lost without you."

That had been the *real* Dr. Jekyll speaking – the master whom Poole had grown, over the years, to admire and respect. In recent months, though, the *real* Dr. Jekyll seemed to have disappeared, his place being taken over by someone else who looked like him, sounded like him, but, in some strange, unfathomable way, wasn't him. Besides, Dr. Jekyll, even the false one, was hardly ever here any more. If he wasn't locked away in the Cabinet until all hours of the night, he was absent from the house entirely. And this new fellow was so often around – this new fellow for whom Poole could spare nothing but a sniff of disapproval. The fellow called...

There was a hammering at the front door.

Poole's right eyebrow rose. It was late for a guest. And guests were a rarity at Dr. Jekyll's house these days. The hammering continued as Poole made his slow way to the door.

He recognized the man on the doorstep. It was Mr. Utterson, the lawyer. He had come here often in the old days, when Dr. Jekyll still entertained a lot. But Poole hadn't seen him for months – and never in such a anxious state. The man's brow was creased with worry.

"Is he here?" gasped Mr. Utterson, as soon as the door was fully open.

"Dr. Jekyll?"

"Yes – Jekyll! Is he here?"

"I believe he is still at work in his dissecting room," said Poole gravely, "although he may have gone out. There is a back door, you see, sir, leading out onto Mitre Street."

"Yes!" cried Utterson, pushing past the butler. "I know all about that door, though I'm beginning to wish I'd never laid eyes on it! I was standing there only a minute ago."

"Perhaps you would take a seat by the fire," said Poole, opening the drawing-room door, "while I go to see if the master is available."

The fire had nearly burned out, but it still seemed welcoming after the cold night air. Utterson couldn't make himself sit down, though; instead he strode backward and forward across the room, rubbing his hands agitatedly together.

Poole was back in a minute. "Dr. Jekyll is not in the house," he said, "and he will not answer my knock at the door of the Cabinet."

"But is he there?" said Utterson urgently.

"I do not believe he is, sir. The place seems deserted."

"But I saw a man go in that door only a minute ago."

"That'll have been Mr. Hyde, sir. He has a key."

"Hyde! Yes, it was him! Your master seems to place a great deal of trust in him, Poole."

"That is true, sir." The butler looked sorrowful. "All of us servants have instructions from Dr. Jekyll to do whatever Mr. Hyde tells us, just as if he were our second master." It was obvious, from the expression on his face, that Poole found this a most lamentable state of affairs.

"You don't like that much, do you, Poole?" said Utterson more gently.

"Dr. Jekyll is an excellent employer," said Poole.

There was a pause.

"I don't believe I have ever met Mr. Hyde myself," said Utterson at last. "It seems strange that Jekyll should not have introduced me to such a close associate."

"Mr. Hyde never dines with us," said Poole. "Dr. Jekyll does not choose to have him around when there are guests here. Indeed, even we servants rarely see Mr. Hyde. He spends most of his time, when he is here, in the Cabinet with Dr. Jekyll working on their experiments together. We are not allowed to disturb them when they are at work. Even the meals the maid leaves on a tray by the door are generally left untouched."

Utterson was thoughtful. "He's an odd fellow, this Mr. Hyde of yours," he said.

"More... more *frightening* than odd, sir," confided Poole, and then realized that he had said too much. "Dr. Jekyll is an excellent employer," he repeated, and Utterson realized he would get no more from the loyal old butler.

On his way home it struck Utterson for the first time that his days as a detective were over: he had found his quarry, so there was no further need for him to haunt the stalls of Mitre Street. He stopped walking for a moment, somewhat saddened by the thought. Then his mind turned back to the problem of Jekyll – and Hyde. He knew his friend had been rather wild in his youth, but that had been decades ago. Surely something he had done then could not be held against him now; no blackmailer could hope to extract money from him by threatening to expose it to the world.

"Yet," he breathed to himself, "while society may forgive deeds done nearly a third of a century ago, God doesn't forget so easily, not God, and perhaps not... other beings." He shook his head. He didn't like where his train of thought was leading. He was a sensible man, an educated nineteenth-century man, not some medieval peasant to be terrified by fears of the dead.

And yet – and yet, there had been that dreadful face, the very sight of which had been enough to freeze his blood. He could believe anything of that face, and of the evil that glowed so visibly behind it. He could believe that... Utterson shook his head again. He was ashamed to admit it, even to himself, but he found it quite easy to believe that Hyde might be a vengeful ghost.

Or even the Devil in person...

Two weeks later, Utterson was surprised to receive a dinner invitation from Jekyll. It had been over a year since Jekyll had shown any signs of wishing to entertain guests. Driven by curiosity as much as anything else, Utterson promptly accepted. The evening passed pleasantly, with a few old friends (Hastie Lanyon was not among them) dining well on the cook's unimaginative but plentiful food, and drinking perhaps too much wine. Jekyll seemed relaxed, cracking jokes and telling tall tales; yet occasionally Utterson thought he saw a look of quiet, rapidly-concealed despair in his friend's eyes.

When the others left, Utterson stayed behind for a final brandy. He and Jekyll chatted lightly for a while and then, when Poole had withdrawn, Utterson got to the point.

"I've been wanting to speak to you for some while, Henry," he said. "It's that will of yours. I don't like it. The thought of it keeps nagging away at me."

"I thought we'd agreed not to talk about that subject any more." Jekyll spoke firmly, yet he was obviously ill at ease. He was a big man with a broad face. Utterson knew he was in his early fifties, and yet he could easily have been mistaken for a man in his mid-thirties had it not been for the silvery greyness of his hair.

Jekyll eventually gave a nervous laugh. "I felt so guilty after I'd left you that day. You were very obviously distressed by the way I had drawn up my will, and I hated to give pain to such an old and dear friend. Yet that is the way it has to be."

"I've learned more about Hyde since then," said Utterson doggedly. "More than I would have wished to, had I known beforehand that —"

"I do not wish to talk about Mr. Hyde," said Jekyll. "Nor about my will. Please can we consider the subject closed."

"I would be a bad friend if I didn't persist." Utterson stared at the brandy swirling in the glass he held. "Has that ghastly man got some hold over you? Does he know some dreadful secret of your past? If that's the case, old chap, you know you can tell me all about it — I can keep a confidence as well as the next man, if not better. If you tell me, I can help you plan how to rid yourself of him."

"You always were the very best of friends, Gabriel," said Jekyll, "and I thank you for wanting to help me. But this is a matter in which you can be of no help at all."

"Is it something *very* dreadful?" said Utterson gravely. Jekyll laughed. There was an edge of hysteria to the laugh. "No," he said. "Oh, no, dear Gabriel.

There's nothing so bad as that. I'm an old fuddy-duddy doctor with no secrets that aren't as fuddy-duddy as I am myself."

"Hyde is not so blameless," said Utterson. "There is one thing that I've been told about him... well, it was abominable."

"Hyde is my associate," said Jekyll crisply. "I am not his master. What he chooses to do outside the walls of my home is no concern of mine."

"But —" began Utterson.

Jekyll held up a hand to silence him. "No, Gabriel. I won't talk about this any longer. The position I'm in is a very difficult one. But I'm not being blackmailed – by Hyde, or by anyone else for that matter. And if it makes you feel happier I can tell you one thing: I can get rid of Mr. Hyde at any moment I choose."

"Then I wish to blazes you would!" said Utterson. "I've met the blighter, you know, and he was –"

"He was horribly rude to you," interrupted Jekyll. "I know. He has a terrible manner and I can only apologize for him."

"These really must be exceptionally important experiments you're conducting," muttered Utterson, "and Hyde must be vital to them if you find it's worth putting up with him."

Jekyll smiled, and this time the smile was genuine. "They're indeed important experiments," he said. "Far more important than I could possibly explain to you, Gabriel."

"Try me."

"No fear," said Jekyll with another broad smile. "I tried to tell Hastie Lanyon about them, and even he – a medical man – failed completely to understand the importance of what Hyde and I are doing. He called me a crackpot. Suggested I should try to gain admittance to a lunatic asylum. And, when I refused, he swept out of the house – and, even though he had been my friend almost as long as you have, dear Gabriel, I have to confess that I was glad to see him go. There is nothing more destructive to scientific progress than a hidebound mind."

Jekyll seemed please with this turn of phrase, for he repeated it softly, rolling the words around his mouth, appreciating them.

"Then it shall be as you say," said Utterson, draining the last of his brandy. "I can't pretend that I like your Mr. Hyde, or that I will ever be able to like him, but your wishes will be obeyed. The terms of your will shall be respected. You have my word."

"Please do that," said Jekyll. "I trust you, Gabriel. If anything should happen to me, I know that you'll see Hyde gets his rights. I beg you, in the name of our friendship, to see that he receives justice."

"I swear to that," said Utterson, thinking: *If anything happens to you, Jekyll old chap, I'll make sure Hyde receives justice all right!*

After Utterson had departed into the night – amid much clapping of shoulders and loud promises to get together again soon – and after Poole and the other servants had gone to bed, Jekyll returned to the drawing room to linger in front of the fire a while longer. If Utterson could have seen the expression that was now on the doctor's face, he might not have agreed so readily to let matters lie. For in place of the earlier calmness, agonized doubt was written clearly across Jekyll's broad features.

"I wish I could be so sure," he said quietly to the dull red embers. "I told Gabriel that I could get rid of Hyde at any moment. I wish I felt as certain as I sounded."

He shuddered. "I might as well wish I could get rid of myself," he continued to himself, letting out a little snort of mirthless laughter. "And that," he added after a pause, "might well be the best way of finishing all this..."

He mused on. "Yet I'm a scientist," he said suddenly, as if trying to justify himself to the dying fire, "and it is my duty to seek out knowledge." The corners of his mouth twitched, but only for a moment.

"Yet if, ten years ago, I had known what I know now..."

Horror on the Embankment

Kate Stewart was in love with William, the footman at Number 27. She knew that it was love because no other emotion in the whole of human experience could possibly compare with what she felt. And that, surely, was the test of love. Sitting by the window of her room, high above the Embankment, overlooking the Thames, Kate played a game with her fingers. Her right hand was to count off the fingers of her left hand, counting "He loves me" for one finger, "He loves me not" for the next, "He loves me" for the one after that, and so on. But the fingers of her left hand kept dodging away from her right, so that she could never tell – *really* she could never tell – how many fingers she would count before the game came to an end. Of course, she was the person who decided when the game *did* come to that end, so perhaps it wasn't so surprising that the last finger to be counted was always "He loves me".

She was seventeen years old, and lucky to have such a secure position: maid to a rich widow. Of course, Mrs. Farquharson could be terribly tiresome at times, but she was a good-hearted old soul and she'd told Kate that her job was secure for as long as she wished it to be. Mrs. Farquharson didn't yet know about William, and might not take kindly to her maid becoming a married woman, but that was a problem Kate would face when she came to it.

Tired of her game for the moment, Kate looked out of the window. There was a bright full moon high in the sky, and the air was frosty clear. The surface of the river was black except where it shone silver with reflections of the streetlamps on the South Bank, and the water seemed almost still.

The Embankment was deserted. It was too cold a night for anyone to venture out who didn't have to.

She was vaguely aware that a hansom cab had passed by a few minutes ago, but otherwise there had been nobody on the street this past half-hour or more.

No – there was someone coming. Pausing from time to time to lean on the parapet by the riverbank, an elderly gentleman was ambling along. He had a dark greatcoat reaching almost to the ground, and around his neck he had a long white woolly scarf. His mane of hair was as silvery as the moonlight. In one hand he carried a light walking stick; with the other he occasionally plucked his pipe from his mouth. Watching him, Kate began to smile: he seemed so very content with the world, even though it was freezing cold, that it made her feel warm inside just to look at him.

And now someone else was approaching from the other direction. Kate frowned. This person didn't give her the same feeling of comfort as the old man with the greatcoat and silvery hair. It was a little man, walking very quickly and busily, so that his body seemed to be all elbows. He didn't have an overcoat on; he was dressed in trousers and tails and a flowing cloak, as if he'd been to a party. He carried a thick walking stick. She couldn't see his face, but she felt certain she wouldn't like it. There was something unsettling about the scuttling figure.

She turned her attention back to the old man leaning on the parapet. He, too, had noticed the fast-moving pedestrian, and had raised his head, removing his pipe from his mouth and smiling in greeting. She could see him speaking, probably saying that it was a fine, fresh night to be out and about.

The little man came up to the older one and stopped abruptly. From the movements of his head she could tell he was saying something very forcefully, perhaps even shouting. From this distance, through the glass of her window, she could hear nothing. The smile was gone from the silver-haired man's face now, replaced by a frown. He put up a hand towards the other, as if to calm him down. Perhaps the little man was a lunatic, walking the streets in that industrious way and stopping to rant at anyone he passed.

Kate was beginning to feel scared. She leaned forward, her breath coming in sharp little panting noises. The glass in front of her steamed up, and she hurriedly wiped the mist away. She gasped when the moonlight revealed the little man's face. But what she saw next was enough to make her faint dead away.

The little man had taken a step back, and now he was raising his heavy walking stick high above his shoulders, and he was bringing it down in a great swooping arc on the head of the silver-haired man, and...

In the distance, leaning against the parapet, Edward Hyde sees an old man, rather too fat for his own good. The first thing he notices about him, though, is not his plumpness but the impressive mane of thick silver hair that covers his head and flows down almost to his shoulders. He is puffing comfortably on a big, curved pipe.

Hyde approaches him swiftly. He has spent the evening drinking and brawling in one of the seedy areas down by the docks, and by all rights he should be exhausted by now. Instead, the deeds he has done this evening have made the blood sing in his veins, so that every part of his body seems to be twitching with life. He feels he needn't rest or sleep for the next century or more; that he's as strong as the world itself. He wishes there were more men to fight, more dogs to set against each other, more mugs of frothing ale to drink, more opium to smoke...

He wants *more* of everything – more, more, more of this glorious exhilaration, this gratification of all the senses, that is called "life".

As he comes close, the fool with the silver hair leers idiotically at him.

"A fine night, my friend!" says the man.

"Finer than you might think!" snaps Hyde. "Too fine to waste time talking about it!"

"I didn't mean to offend," says the old man in a placatory fashion, half-turning away.

But then the man turns back again, wrinkling up his eyes as he peers at Hyde's face. "Good lord! I didn't recognize you for a moment. You're... But no, now I look again I see you're not. You're much too young to be him. It was just a trick of the light. I'm so sorry." He smiles again, and lifts a hand in apology.

All of a sudden Hyde is full of contempt for this fat, complacent old buffoon. Seven decades this fool must have occupied space on earth, and through all of that time he cannot have felt even a breath of the *life* that Hyde has come to expect every second to bring him.

Somewhere in a far corner of his mind a small voice is telling him that this is no smug, idle old fool but Sir Danvers Carew M.P., one of the few respected politicians in the land — the man who single-handedly forced the government to give greater help to the poor and the homeless. But Hyde ignores that little voice in the shouting rush of his uncontrollable contempt and anger.

Besides, Carew has half-recognized him...

"Get out of my way!" snarls Hyde.

Carew frowns perplexedly.

"But I'm not *in* your way, dear fellow," he says. "This pavement is wide enough for a dozen to walk side by side." Then his face relaxes into the artificial smile of someone who thinks he's dealing with a madman. "But if it would make you happier, my friend, I'll press myself a little closer to the parapet..."

He leans forward to touch Hyde reassuringly on the shoulder.

That's the last straw!

Feeling a curious vitality surging through every part of him, Hyde swings up his heavy walking stick, faster than the speed of thought, and brings it crashing down on Sir Danvers Carew's silver-haired head. The sound of that terrible blow seems to echo along the fronts of the blank-faced houses on the other side of the street.

Carew drops to his knees, letting his cane fall to one side. He lifts his hands up to his head, where the silver hair is already blotted dark with blood in the moonlight. A wheezing groan comes from his mouth. Hyde brings his stick down again. This second blow, even more forceful than the first, kills Carew instantly, and he slumps over to one side.

Hyde cannot stop himself. His mind seems to be filled with an angry mob chanting: "Kill! Kill! *Kill!*" He thrashes downwards with the stick, this time reversed so that its heavy silver handle sinks into the dead man's face. He knows he is making little yipping noises of glee as he carries on raining blows down on the motionless body. He almost wishes that his yelps would attract attention, and that someone would come running to the scene, for his appetite for blood suddenly seems greater than any appetite he has ever known...

Kate came around to find herself stretched across the floor. She pulled herself to her knees, shaking her head muzzily. She must have fallen asleep sitting at the window and dreaming of William, she concluded. It had been a long, hard day – Mrs. Farquharson had been particularly demanding because of her asthma – and Kate must have been more tired than she thought.

Her candle had burned away completely. Moving clumsily, she undressed in the dark and put on her nightgown, then climbed into her narrow bed.

Images spun through her head – vivid pictures drawn from the dreadful nightmare she had had while lying on the floor. An old man with silver hair suddenly turning dark...

She shivered, and not just from the cold of the sheets. That nightmare had been very... realistic.

Telling herself she was being silly, she slipped out of bed again and tiptoed to the window.

There was a dark form spread across the pavement on the far side of the street. Even from here the shape looked broken.

That was when she began to scream.

Gabriel Utterson was eating his breakfast when the message came. Molyneaux gave him the hand-delivered letter, and Utterson scanned it as he crunched on a slice of toast and ginger marmalade. As his eye drifted downwards, his body stiffened, and he laid the rest of the toast on his plate.

There was a second letter tucked inside the first. Although the envelope had been stamped, the letter had not been posted. The envelope was addressed to Utterson, and he quickly opened it. The letter was from Sir Danvers Carew, whom he had known casually for years and whom he occasionally served as lawyer. It was an invitation to come to the Houses of Parliament for coffee the following Tuesday. Utterson turned it over in his hands, looking for anything else, but there was nothing except, on the envelope, a tiny smear of blood.

The policeman who had brought the message was waiting with Molyneaux in the hall.

"We must go immediately," said Utterson. "Do you have a carriage ready?"

"It's waiting outside," said the young policeman. "Inspector Newcomen did say as it was urgent that you, er..."

"Quite, quite!" said Utterson hurriedly. "Molyneaux, my coat, my hat and my gloves!"

The butler had them ready, and Utterson swiftly put them on. A moment later he was rattling along Gaunt Street in the police carriage, with the young constable sitting beside him.

"Is it really Sir Danvers Carew?" said the lawyer.

"We're not certain," said the constable uneasily. "The head was so badly beaten that it's hard to distinguish the face. We thought that you, as a friend of his might..."

The constable broke off. Utterson glanced sideways and saw that the young man was looking sick.

They were soon at Strand Police Station, and Newcomen was shaking Utterson's hand. "Thank you so much for coming, sir," said the detective. He and the lawyer had met each other several times before in the course of their duties. "This is a ghastly business."

Utterson was shown downstairs to the mortuary. The air smelled of damp and death. He felt his half-

eaten breakfast shifting unsteadily in his stomach. An attendant pulled back a bloodstained sheet from a body laid out on a low table.

The lawyer had seen death before, but never like this. He turned away, his eyes stinging sharply. Newcomen put an arm around his shoulders.

"I'll be all right in a moment," Utterson gasped.

It took longer than a moment, but at last he was able to turn and look at the corpse again. The head was a mess of blood and silver hair. Only the nose had survived intact, and Utterson recognized the prominent aquiline beak of Sir Danvers. Gesturing to the attendant to pull the sheet down further, Utterson saw the broad gold wedding ring the politician had always worn.

"That's Sir Danvers Carew, all right," he said in a choked voice.

"He had a birthmark on the back of his right hand. Would you be so kind as to... ?"

The attendant turned the hand over, and there among the bruises was the cherry-red blob that Utterson remembered.

"It's him," he said. "But who could have done this? The man didn't have an enemy in the..."

He paused. Carew's campaigns on behalf of the poor had earned him enemies among the rich, who begrudged the increased taxes they had to pay. But this was surely not enough to drive anyone to murder.

"Come upstairs," said the detective gently. "There's something else we want to show you."

Newcomen's office was tiny, barely more than a cubicle, and full of books. The detective showed Utterson to an upright chair, then shifted piles of paper to clear a space on his desk. He sat down himself.

"There was an eyewitness," he said once the two men had settled. "A maid in one of the nearby houses was at her window, and saw the whole thing."

"Then..."

"She knew the attacker. She'd seen him before when he'd come calling on her mistress, a Mrs. Farquharson. She says she didn't recognize him at all until the very last moment, and then she fainted."

"She's certain?" said Utterson. "If she fainted right afterwards she might be confused."

"She's an intelligent lass, is young Kate," said Newcomen, his weaselly face cracking into a smile. "And an observant one, although she seems not to have noticed the kind of activities her mistress engaged in. The man that she saw was probably a customer for Mrs. Farquharson's opium. And it's an old rule that where there's opium there's likely to be murder, sooner or later."

"Where there's opium there's likely *not* to be Gabriel Utterson," said the older man primly. "There should be a law against the stuff. Presumably this was some rogue from the docks?"

"No," said Newcomen. "Mrs. Farquharson's customers come from among what society chooses to call 'the gentry'. The attacker was what passes for a gentleman. A Mr. Hyde."

Suddenly Utterson's mind was thrown back a full year, to the conversation he had had with Jekyll in which the doctor had said he could rid himself of Hyde at any moment. Could it be the same Hyde?

"Is he a small man, all elbows and motion?" he said. "With a face that... a face that you don't much like to look at?" he ended lamely.

"You could have taken the words right out of Kate's mouth," said Newcomen, leaning forward earnestly. "What do you know of Mr. Hyde? And do you recognize this?"

He pulled the upper half of a walking stick from beneath his desk and laid it on the surface. The thick stick was splintered where it had broken in the middle. There was still some blood on its heavy handle, which was made of silver and shaped in the form of a devil's head.

"I do indeed," said Utterson slowly. "I bought it myself, ten, maybe twelve, years ago. It was a present to a friend of mine."

"To Mr. Hyde?"

"No. Someone else. I don't want to drag his name into this unless I must."

"You may have to."

"Yes, but not yet."

Newcomen was visibly dissatisfied.

"But," said Utterson, "I have Hyde's address – at least, the address where he was living a year ago. I have it written down in my notebook."

"I must go there at once," said Newcomen. He leapt to his feet.

"I'll come with you," said Utterson, remembering his promise to Jekyll. "Although I've met the swine only once, I seem accidentally to have become his lawyer."

Newcomen raised his eyebrows in curiosity, but made no comment.

Twenty minutes later, the police carriage drew up in front of the shabby house at Number 43 Staplers' Gate, Soho. Utterson looked around as he climbed down from the carriage. There were heaps of windblown litter wherever he looked. The window of the café on the corner had been broken during the night, probably by one of the empty bottles rolling around on the pavement. This was not a part of London he came to often, and every time he did so he was reminded why his visits were so rare. Although it was nine o'clock in the morning, it seemed as if it were twilight, for there was already a heavy brown fog crouching over London. Utterson shuddered.

Newcomen moved rapidly ahead of him to the door of Number 43, gesturing to a constable to position himself at the side of the door. Clearly the detective wasn't taking any chances. Utterson had seen Newcomen issuing revolvers to two of his men before they left Strand Police Station. Briefly he wondered if he himself might be in any danger but, dismissing the thought as fanciful, he joined Newcomen at the door.

It was opened by an elderly woman. She peered up at them through bloodshot eyes.

"Is this the residence of one Mr. Edward Hyde?" said Newcomen pompously.

"It is," she said. Utterson had the feeling that she was looking them both over to see if either showed signs of being profitable. "He's been a lodger here these past two years. Are you friends of his?"

"Perhaps, if he's an honest man," said the detective.

Utterson broke in. "This is Inspector Newcomen of Scotland Yard," he explained. "You must tell him as much as you know, about Mr. Hyde."

"I don't see as there's much I can tell," she said, wringing her hands together. Her eyes were now evasive, darting here and there, looking everywhere except at the faces of the two men. "He keeps himself to himself, does Mr. Hyde. Not that we see him all that often. Sometimes months go by when he's not here, then he just suddenly turns up, like he did last night."

"Last night?" said Newcomen eagerly. "What time was this?"

The woman looked at him as if wondering whether he would pay her a sovereign for the information.

"I'm a police officer, madam," Newcomen reminded her, and her face fell.

"He came in very late," she said. "And very noisy. He woke me up. He ran up the stairs and slammed his door shut, and then he was busy there doing something. But I gets back to sleep somehow. Only to be woke up by him again a bit later when he goes out again, every bit as loud as the last time."

"What hour was this?" said Utterson.

She shrugged her thin shoulders under her grimy wool shawl. "Can't say. Never been much of a one for clocks, myself."

"We must see his rooms," said Utterson, turning to Newcomen.

"Can't be allowed, it can't," said the landlady. "Those rooms is Mr. Hyde's, and he's always told me most special that no one but him's allowed in there."

"This is a police matter," the detective said. "I insist."

All at once her face was wreathed in a gloating grin. "He's in bad trouble, then, is he?"

"He might be," said Utterson, coughing into his hand. "We don't know for certain yet."

The house seemed almost derelict. The old woman led them up the uncarpeted stairs to the first-floor landing. "Mr. Hyde has the two rooms on this floor," she explained, fumbling a large key from the pocket of her flannel skirt. "They connects," she added. "And the bathroom on the floor above is his as well."

Newcomen let out a slight whistle of astonishment as the woman pushed the door open, but Utterson found himself curiously unsurprised. There could have been no greater contrast with the unpainted landing. The room was shelved on three sides with books, while the fourth had a long mahogany table set beneath the window and an easy chair beside it. The men's feet were silent as they ventured across the thick-pile carpet towards the inner door, which they soon discovered led into an untidy bedroom. The walls of this second room were covered in pictures. Some were of the sort that Utterson would not have permitted into his own home, but all were of the finest quality; although he was no expert, he was willing to swear that one of them was a Rembrandt.

"He's not short of a quid or two, our Mr. Hyde," muttered Newcomen.

"There's a fortune in paintings here," Utterson confirmed.

"And a fortune in wine, too," said Newcomen, pointing at the open door of a closet; through the door, Utterson saw dozens of neatly stacked bottles. Moving his gaze, he saw that all the drawers of the chest had been pulled out onto the floor; a few socks and a dirty shirt lay on the crumpled bedclothes. It looked as if Hyde had hurriedly packed and fled.

The Inspector moved back into the main room and went to examine the fireplace. This was built into one of the walls of bookshelves, and Utterson wondered about the risk of accident. Newcomen was crouched down, sifting with his fingers through the ashes in the hearth.

"What have we here?" Newcomen asked. Shaking off cinders, he held up the remains of a chequebook. "Looks like he was trying to make part of his life disappear altogether," he said, "but was in too much of a hurry to do the job properly."

He opened the chequebook and blew on it. Soot rose. "Gilvey's Bank," he read. "My officers will pay a call there and see what they can find out. Too early for the banks to be open yet, so maybe my boys will get a nice surprise when Mr. Hyde drops in to clear out his account." His smile transformed his thin features. "If we're in luck."

"I shouldn't think you will be," said Utterson sourly. "Mr. Hyde may be many things, but I don't think he's stupid. That's certainly not the impression I've gained of him."

"You may be right," said the Inspector, "but he doesn't seem to have been clever enough to take the other half of the murder weapon away with him."

Utterson followed the detective's gaze and saw, propped up against the books behind the door, the broken-off lower part of the walking stick he had given Jekyll so many years before.

"Ah," he said thoughtfully. "I imagine this creates enough of a case against Hyde – my client – for you to be able to issue a warrant for his arrest."

"Yes, indeed," said Newcomen, grinning. "I should think this discovery just about wraps up the case. We'll launch a manhunt for Hyde" – Utterson noticed that the detective had stopped calling him Mr. Hyde – "and have him in the cells before nightfall."

"Assuming he hasn't left London," said the lawyer.

Newcomen's grin slipped a little, but he tried to conceal it. "Yes, sir," he said. "Assuming that's the case. But that would have meant leaving behind all the money in his bank account, which according to this chequebook is nearly seven hundred pounds. No, I should think we'll nail him at the bank, sir."

"We'll see," breathed Utterson.

It was late in the afternoon before Utterson could rid himself of the police, and all the time he was worried that Newcomen would suddenly remember to ask him about the friend to whom he had admitted having given the walking-stick. But the detective had plenty on his mind, and as the day progressed his face grew steadily gloomier. No one of Hyde's description had turned up at Gilvey's Bank, and, although police were combing the streets of London in an ever-widening circle around Staplers' Gate, they were hampered by the lack of any picture – or even a clear description – of the man they were hunting. All anyone could say, including Utterson himself and the keen-eyed Kate Stewart, was that Hyde's face had no particularly distinguishing features except for the fact that even to glance at it was enough to make you feel you were in the presence of a very great evil. Everything else paled beside that: it was impossible to remember what Hyde actually looked like.

When Utterson finally asked if he were free to go, Newcomen dismissed him rudely, as if glad to see the back of him.

The fog had lifted. The lawyer went straight to Jekyll's house and beat impatiently with his cane on the heavy wooden door. Poole appeared almost immediately.

"I must see your master," growled Utterson. "At once. I don't care a fig if he's up to his eyes in another of those blasted experiments of his — I need to see him right now."

"He is indeed in the Cabinet," said Poole.

"Then take me there!"

"At once, sir. If you will follow me."

Utterson had seen the back yard many times from the upstairs windows, but this was the first time he had been in it. He was dimly aware of orderly vegetable beds, but his attention was focused on the smaller building on the other side of the yard. A few worn steps led up to a green-painted door. The walls of the little building were of plain brick, blackened by the years. There was a single small window covered in grey grime; by comparison with the rest, one part shone where someone had been wiping at the glass.

"So that's the famous Cabinet," said Utterson.

"It is," said Poole. The old butler climbed the wooden stairs and knocked timidly at the door.

There was a mumble from inside.

"It is Mr. Utterson," said Poole in response to the mumble. "He says he must see you right away."

Another mumble.

"He insists that it is urgent."

"Tell him I won't go away until I've seen him," said Utterson.

Poole repeated something of this to the door. At last there was the sound of a bolt being drawn back. Henry Jekyll appeared in the doorway.

Utterson was aghast. His friend looked as if he had aged twenty years. The wrinkles of his broad face (surely there hadn't been nearly so many of them before?) showed the marks of recent tears. His eyes were wide and flickering. He was jacketless and tieless, and his shirt was torn at the collar. If Utterson had seen him in the street he might not have recognized him, but hurried on by.

"Good heavens, Henry!" the lawyer exclaimed. "What on earth has happened to you?"

"It's not what's happened to me," said the doctor hoarsely. "It's what's happened to poor old Danvers Carew. I heard the newsboys calling it in the square."

"Then you must know that the police are seeking Edw..." began Utterson, then remembered that Poole was still with them.

"Yes," said Jekyll. "I heard the rest of it. Poole, perhaps you should go indoors now."

The butler bowed slightly and left them.

"Come into the dissecting room," said Jekyll wearily.

Utterson followed him into the Cabinet and found himself in a fully equipped laboratory. He was not a man of science – indeed, he carefully cultivated as much ignorance as possible of scientific matters – but the place seemed to him to represent a considerable amount of money. There were two or three gleaming machines, the function of which Utterson could not even begin to guess. Over in the corner was a cumbersome device made of metal and coils of wire, and Utterson deduced this must be one of those electricity-generating machines he had read about in the newspapers, for further wires led in a tangle from it to the other gadgets that crowded at one end of the laboratory bench.

The table was covered with numerous flasks, stands, jars and bottles, as well as leather-bound books and notepads. Two walls of the dissecting room were lined with glass-fronted dressers containing countless little corked bottles of powders and liquids. A fire-axe hung from a hook behind the door, and a bucket of sand was on the floor beneath it.

At the far end of the room, three steps rose to a door covered in red fabric. It was partly open, and Utterson could see that on the other side of it was a smaller room where a fire crackled brightly in the hearth. The vigorous flames seemed out of place: the dissecting room was otherwise filled with the air of bleak despair.

Jekyll led him up to the smaller room. "This is the Cabinet proper, although we've adopted the habit of using that name for the whole building," he said, warming his hands as Utterson sat in an armchair.

"My predecessor in this house, a doctor like myself, had this outhouse built so that he could teach his students the principles of anatomy. He lectured downstairs in the dissecting room, cutting up the cadavers, and retreated here to the Cabinet when he wanted to do his own private reading and research. Unlike him, I do no dissection, so I have turned the surgical theatre into a chemical laboratory. But still I like to read and relax in this room where no one will disturb me."

"No one except Edward Hyde," said Utterson heavily. "Stop beating about the bush, Henry. You know why I've come."

"I do indeed," said Jekyll sadly.

"Is he here?"

Jekyll took a moment to reply. "No," he said eventually.

"I didn't like that pause," said Utterson. "Let me make myself plain, Henry. You're a long-established client of mine, and have been a friend for even longer than that. But Carew was my friend and client as well, and I am determined to see his murderer brought to justice. Even if I had loathed the very sight of Carew I'd want to see the killer seized. No man should die the way that Carew did. I've seen the body! Hyde must have gone berserk!"

"Hyde isn't here," said Jekyll. "I swear to that. And I swear that I shall never set eyes on him again. You have my word. The world shall never be troubled by him again." He spoke bitterly.

"How can you know this?" demanded Utterson.

"I've had a letter from him. It came this morning. I've spent all day wondering whether I should burn it or hand it over to the police. I was just on the verge of deciding that the wisest course would be to give it to you, as my lawyer, when you arrived." Jekyll took a folded sheet of paper from the mantel and passed it to Utterson.

The letter was short, and written in spidery handwriting that, without his glasses, Utterson found hard to decipher:

My dear Jekyll,

By the time you read this I shall be far away. For these past two years I have repaid your constant generosity with nothing but selfishness. But this time I have gone too far. I have done something despicable and vile. The police would hang me if they caught me, and would be right to do so, but I have a powerful affection for this miserable life of mine and so will not give them the chance. The place where I am going is far from the reach of the law, and I shall be safe among friends there. All that I regret is that I shall never again look upon the face of the best friend I ever had: Dr. Henry Jekyll.

Your unworthy associate and sorry friend,

Edward Hyde

"Do you have the envelope?" said Utterson when he had finished reading.

Jekyll shrugged unhappily.

"I threw it on the fire before I realized what the letter was about," he said. "But there was no postmark, I do remember that much. Hyde must have shoved it through the letterbox himself before the household awoke this morning."

"And you don't know whether you should give it to the police or burn it," said Utterson. "To tell you the truth, Henry," he continued, rubbing his eyes with the back of his hand, "I don't know either. If you haven't any objections, I'll hang on to the letter and decide tomorrow what would be best."

"I would be very grateful if you did that, Gabriel," said Jekyll. "I... I seem to have lost all confidence in my own judgment."

"Tell me one more thing," said Utterson as he rose to his feet, putting the folded letter carefully into his breast pocket. "That confounded will of yours – it was Hyde who dictated its terms to you, wasn't it?"

Jekyll looked pale. "Yes. It was."

"I knew it!" exclaimed Utterson. "It was what I was afraid of! The scoundrel meant to murder you, in due course, and inherit everything you had. What on earth was the hold he had over you, Henry, that you agreed to draw up that infernal document?"

"That is behind me now," said Jekyll firmly. Although the voice was quiet, Utterson could see in the set of the doctor's jaw that there was no point in asking him anything more. The secret was one that Jekyll would take to his grave.

"I shall call on you tomorrow," Utterson said stiffly. "I'll tell you of any decision I make about this letter before I do anything else."

"Thank you, Gabriel," said Jekyll, sinking into the armchair and burying his face in his hands. "Thank you for... for everything."

That night Utterson asked Mr. Guest, his clerk, to come and have a drink with him before going home. Guest was a man whom Utterson trusted completely, and he didn't feel he was betraying any faith with Jekyll in asking the clerk to take a look at the letter.

Guest made a hobby out of studying handwriting, and it was possible he might notice something which Utterson had missed.

Briefly he recounted to Guest the circumstances that had brought the letter into his possession.

"There was one odd thing," he concluded. "As I was leaving Dr. Jekyll's house I asked Poole, the butler, if he had seen the person who left the letter, and he told me there had been no post for the house at all today. I pressed him about it, but he was quite insistent: there had been nothing."

"The letter could have been delivered through the door in Mitre Court," Guest observed.

"Yes," said Utterson slowly.

"I suppose that's probably the case. But the thought nags at the back of my mind that the letter might even have been written in the Cabinet itself. Hyde had a key to the place. Chances are he still does. Perhaps Jekyll made him write the letter before he fled – maybe my old friend was lying to me. A couple of years ago I would have trusted my life to the word of Henry Jekyll. It's a sad thing to admit that I'm no longer so certain." He sighed.

Guest took the letter and looked at it closely. "This writing is very distinctive," he said. "Rather *too* distinctive, if you see what I mean."

Utterson looked blank.

"As if it had been forged by someone who was trying to make the handwriting look as different as possible from his own," explained Guest. "It's something you can't do. If you want to produce handwriting that isn't like your own, the best thing is to change just a few things – the way you cross your 't's or dot your 'i's, for example. If you try to make it look entirely different, you almost certainly retain certain distinguishing marks that anyone interested in the subject will be able to recognize."

"Does that handwriting make you think of anyone in particular?" said Utterson, suddenly gripped by dread.

"I mightn't have noticed if we hadn't been talking about Jekyll," said Guest. "If I could perhaps make a comparison, to satisfy myself?"

Utterson went downstairs to his office and fetched a note that Jekyll had sent him some months earlier.

"Yes," said Guest slowly, carefully examining the two sheets side by side. "It's as I thought. Look here at the swash of the 's'. And the capital 'B' is almost identical."

He went on to point out some more similarities, but Utterson had already heard enough.

"This is an interesting exercise," he said. "But of course it cannot prove anything."

Guest, glancing up, saw the expression on the old lawyer's face and hurried to agree. "No proof that any court of law would accept," he said. "Yes, of course it wouldn't be sensible to spread my ideas on the subject around as I might all too easily be wrong. I suggest that we keep these... these suppositions to ourselves, Mr. Utterson."

"I had come to precisely the same conclusion myself," said the lawyer. "If we spoke about this to anyone else, an innocent man's name might well be brought into disrepute! That would be terrible!"

"Too, too terrible," murmured Guest. "Too terrible to contemplate."

But both men knew that they weren't deceiving themselves, and after the clerk had left, Utterson remained up for a long time, worrying and chewing at his nails.

"Henry Jekyll forging for a murderer!" he said over and over to himself. "What ghastliness would force him to do that?" And his mind conjured up images of frightful crimes.

What had Jekyll done?

The question dogged him for the next eight weeks.

Dr. Lanyon's Terror

Hyde looks around the dissecting room with a gleam of satisfaction in his eyes. It is so long since he has been here – how long, he cannot tell, but it seems to him as if it has been almost forever. He swears savagely, cursing the name of the man who has for so long kept him imprisoned in the cell of nonexistence: Dr. Henry Jekyll.

Then his mood changes abruptly, and there is a skip in his step as he goes up the stairs to the Cabinet. The wallpaper hides the door of a cupboard in the corner. He opens it and pulls out a gentleman's black dress suit, a dusty black top hat, a pair of scuffed black shoes, a dirty white shirt and a dilapidated black bow-tie. He fumbles a bit longer in the cupboard, seeking the walking stick that always used to be there, and then dimly recalls breaking it. He cackles as the memory becomes clearer. Who would have thought the old man to have so much blood in him?

Soon he is dressed. He looks at himself in the mirror over the fireplace, and is evidently very satisfied with what he sees. He feels so full of life. He finds some money – fifty or more pounds in notes – in his trouser pocket, and riffles through it gleefully. One of the very first things he must do tonight is buy himself a new walking stick; something a little stronger than the last one.

Coming back down into the dissecting room, he looks around him, and then giggles. There's the very thing! He picks up the metal stand from Jekyll's laboratory bench and hefts it in his hand. Its lead base is suitably heavy. He strips the clamps quickly off the upright shaft, and tests the stand for balance again. It won't be much use as a walking stick, of course, but in case he should feel a sudden, uncontrollable desire to *hit* someone...

He pauses a second, puzzled. Always before he has awoken to find an emptied beaker on the laboratory bench, but today there isn't one. It's not a matter of any importance, of course, but it's a variation from the routine and, as such, unsettling. He frowns a moment, then decides to forget the whole thing.

Hyde lets himself out into Mitre Court. It's very late at night and there doesn't seem to be anyone else around; even so, he shuts the door quietly behind him, for fear of attracting the attention of the servants in the main building.

As he finishes locking the door, a small tabby cat comes up and starts rubbing itself against his leg. He bends down to tickle it behind one ear, and it arches its neck backwards in pleasure, purring loudly. Putting down the laboratory stand carefully, he picks the cat up in both hands and holds it so that its yellow eyes are level with his own. He giggles again.

Then he clutches the cat to his face and bites out its throat.

"The master is not home," said Poole.

"But he *must* be home!" cried Utterson. "I have his invitation here in my hand!"

The butler abandoned his loftiness. "Dr. Jekyll has not been entirely himself recently, Mr. Utterson," he confided.

"He seemed healthy enough last Thursday, when I dined here with Lanyon," said Utterson. "At least let me in out of the rain, man!"

Poole stepped aside so that Utterson could come into the hall. "It's been just these past few days," said the butler. "He's hardly been in the house, day or night, and when we've seen him he's looked like he's kissed Death itself, he has. Most of his time he spends in the Cabinet, and how often he comes and goes from there through the Mitre Court door we have no idea. But I knocked at the Cabinet door just five minutes ago and there was no reply."

Utterson thought rapidly. Poole hadn't said the name, but it was clear he was thinking it: *Edward Hyde*. For the past two months Jekyll had seemed to be free of the loathsome man's malevolent influence, and had rejoined the social circle he had so long deserted, dining with friends, throwing parties, going to the theatre. But, from what Poole had just said, it sounded terribly as if Hyde were back, despite Jekyll's promise.

"Have you seen Mr. Hyde?" said Utterson.

"No, sir. Not a trace of him."

"Well, that's a relief." Utterson drew a hand across his brow.

"Although," he continued, "that's no guarantee he hasn't returned. He could just be taking more care to conceal himself."

"I'm afraid so, sir."

Utterson grunted. During these past two months, while the police had been searching for Hyde, the newspapers had been full of details about the evil little man's career of crime. No, "crime" wasn't really the right word. The things that he had done were characterized not so much by lawbreaking as by malice. He had enjoyed the creation of pain and misery. He was like a child who had never grown out of pulling the wings off flies, but had become an adult who liked pulling the limbs off cats and dogs – and even people. The police now thought he was responsible for at least six other murders in addition to that of Sir Danvers Carew; two of his victims had been hideously mutilated after death. Elsewhere there were broken lives, and people who would wear the scars inflicted by Edward Hyde for the rest of their days.

At nights, Utterson prayed to be forgiven for wishing for the news that Hyde was dead.

Utterson's mind went back to the forged letter. It still lay in his safe. After much thought, he had decided not to hand it over to the police. Now he wondered if he had been wise.

"Let's hope that Hyde hasn't come back to haunt us, eh, Poole?" he said, trying to sound cheerful.

"I hope not indeed, sir."

"Tell Dr. Jekyll I've called," added Utterson, turning to the door.

"I shall indeed, sir."

On the pavement Utterson mused for a moment or two. For the sake of his friendship with Jekyll, he had kept matters from the police for too long. It was time he confessed everything. It was his civic duty. If Jekyll had renewed his association with Hyde, then he had deliberately set himself outside the boundaries of friendship. If Jekyll were innocent, then the intervention of the police would be at worst an embarrassment. Utterson felt as if he had been wandering aimlessly around a maze these last few months, and that now a door had opened to show him the correct route to the heart of the problem.

Yes, he must go and see Inspector Newcomen. At the very least the detective would surely put some men around the house, with instructions to keep a specially close watch on the door in Mitre Court, in case Hyde did choose to come back. Utterson hailed a cab and asked the driver to take him to Strand Police Station.

Two hours later, Dr. Hastie Lanyon was deep in a book when his butler disturbed him.

"A hand-delivered letter, sir," said the man.

"At this time of night?" said Lanyon, taking it.

"I heard it land on the mat just a few moments ago," said the butler.

Lanyon tore open the letter and read it:

Dear Hastie,

I need to ask you to help me. I want you to do as I wish without asking any questions. Believe me, my reputation and probably my very life depend on your prompt assistance.

There are some drugs I need urgently from my house, but for reasons I cannot explain I cannot fetch them myself. By means of a message delivered not long before this one, I have instructed my butler, Poole, to call a locksmith to my house. I want you to go there and, with Poole and the locksmith, break open the door of my Cabinet. But you alone must go inside.

You will find a glass-fronted cabinet just to the left of the door. I think it is unlocked but, if it isn't, please break into it. The drugs I require are all in the fourth drawer from the top. Please bring away with you the entire drawer and its contents, and take them back to your house in Cavendish Square. If you act as soon as you receive this note, you should be home by eleven o'clock.

At midnight, a man will come to your house. Please be alone in your consulting room by that time. Give him the drawer and he will go. Your part in this whole miserable business will be over.

I know these requests will seem bizarre to you, but please be reassured that I have not lost my senses — or, at least, not in this respect. Should you decide you cannot agree to my requests, however, then, my dear Hastie, madness will be the very least of the things that I have to fear.

Your good friend, a man in need —

Henry Jekyll

"Jekyll must be crazy," muttered Lanyon under his breath. "I've never heard of such a..."

Yet Jekyll had been his old self of late — and Lanyon had known him for so many years.

He looked up at his butler. "Call me a cab," he said. "I have to go out for a while."

Barely a quarter of an hour later he was at Jekyll's house. He found that Poole and the locksmith, a burly fellow named Baldwin, were waiting for him, just as Jekyll's letter had said they would be. As the butler let him in, Lanyon had the uncomfortable sensation that someone was watching him, but when he turned around to look there was no one there except a uniformed constable strolling past on the other side of the street.

The door to the Cabinet was stronger than it looked. Lanyon had wondered why Jekyll should have gone to the trouble of hiring a locksmith when it would have been just as easy to break the door down, but as soon as he examined it he realized that the door was built so as to be virtually indestructible: two men with pickaxes might have been able to force a way in, but only by reducing the door to matchwood.

It took nearly an hour for Baldwin to open the lock, which was as well-made as the door. Lanyon kept glancing at his pocket-watch, fretting over the delay. At this rate he would be lucky to get home by eleven o'clock, and he began to worry about being in time for his mysterious midnight appointment with Jekyll's nameless associate.

Once the door was open, however, everything went very quickly. The glass-fronted chest that Jekyll had mentioned stood open, and it took Lanyon only moments to pull out the fourth drawer and wrap it up carefully in a sheet supplied by Poole. The cab, which he had kept waiting all this time, rattled him home briskly to Cavendish Square, and he was inside with the doors closed behind him just as the church clock began to toll eleven.

Once he had taken off his coat and gloves, he instructed the servants to go to bed and carried the drawer, still wrapped up, into his consulting room. Jekyll's letter hadn't actually forbidden him to look at the stuff in the drawer, and his curiosity was aroused.

He was disappointed. There were several bottles of different powders. He sniffed at these, hoping to be able to identify them, but, apart from guessing that one of them contained bicarbonate of soda among its ingredients, he had no idea what the chemicals could be. There was also a corked jar containing a clear, blood-red liquid, which moved sludgily as he turned the container around. He pulled out the cork and then instantly rammed it tightly back into place as the liquid's eye-watering fumes reached him. Once he could focus clearly again, he peered at the liquid warily through the glass of the jar. That single whiff of powerful fumes told him that the mixture probably contained phosphorus and ether, but obviously there were a number of other substances in there as well.

Without subjecting the stuff to a full chemical analysis, he had no way of finding out what these were, but there could be no doubt that the mixture was poisonous.

The drawer also contained papers and a leather notebook. Lanyon opened it eagerly, recognizing it as Jekyll's notes of his experiments. Perhaps here he would find an explanation for his friend's frequently odd conduct over the past couple of years.

But he was disappointed once again. Page after page was filled with nothing but columns of dates, most of which had some cryptic comment beside them. "Double," said one. "Total failure!!!" said another. The first date was for nearly ten years ago; the last, with another "Total failure!!!" recorded beside it, was for just under a year ago.

After that the pages of the notebook were blank. It looked as if Jekyll had wasted nine years of his time on a series of experiments that had come to nothing.

Lanyon had learned very little from the contents of the drawer. But the fact that they seemed innocent disturbed him: why should Jekyll set up this cloak-and-dagger arrangement with him? He could just as easily have sent his nameless messenger to his own home to fetch the materials he needed. Come to that, why hadn't Jekyll done it himself?

After worrying away at these questions for a few minutes, Lanyon rummaged through a cabinet until he found his old army revolver and a few rounds of ammunition. As he loaded the gun he realized he didn't know whether it would still fire, or even whether it would blow up in his face. But, he reasoned, anyone threatening him wouldn't know that either.

Lanyon settled himself in the chair usually reserved for his patients. The drawer and its contents were hidden under the sheet on the table in front of him. The revolver was stuffed behind the chair's cushion.

He didn't have long to wait. As St. Gregory's sounded out midnight, there was a timid knock on the front door. Lanyon hauled himself to his feet and went to let Jekyll's messenger in.

He had hardly opened the door when a little man sprang in and slammed it shut behind him.

"Where is it?"

"In my consulting room, as Jekyll demanded," said Lanyon. "Why all the urgency?"

"Where is it? Where is it?"

The man shoved him aside and scampered through the door to the consulting room.

"Now just wait a minute!" said Lanyon angrily, as he followed. "I deserve some sort of an explanation! What the devil's going on?"

Coming into the light of the consulting room, he saw the visitor's face clearly for the first time, and before he could stop himself he recoiled. He had often seen faces twisted by the final stages of disease,

but he could not recall ever having seen anyone quite so... quite so *loathsome* before.

The man, who had been pacing agitatedly around the consulting room, paused mid–stride.

"You're quite right," he said. His rasping voice was sinister, but it was obvious he was doing his best to be polite.

"You're certainly owed that explanation, Hastie. But first – where is the drawer Dr. Jekyll asked you to fetch?"

Lanyon's eyes narrowed. He had never met this person before, yet the stranger had the impertinence to address him by his first name, as if they were close friends. Jekyll kept some odd company. Utterson had let slip, a few weeks ago, that old Henry had even been acquainted with that villain Hyde...

That villain Hyde! Who, according to all the newspaper reports, was a little man with an evil light in his eyes! Who moved quickly and jerkily, and who spoke in an unpleasant, rasping voice! *Who had slaughtered Sir Danvers Carew and had probably butchered six other people!*

"The drawer is here," said Lanyon, feeling his heart thumping inside his chest. He tugged the sheet back and, the moment Hyde's attention was distracted, plunged his hand down behind the cushion, grabbing his revolver. He yanked it up to point it at the little man, wishing his hand didn't shake so much.

Hyde froze. "What is this?"

"You can have the drawer once you tell me what's going on."

The man's face suddenly twisted with pain. There was a savage grinding noise, and Lanyon realized with horror that it came from Hyde's mouth: his jaw was gnashing in anguish. Hyde's hand went to his heart, and now his face was turning purple, his eyes wet with tears.

"F-f-for God's sake, Hastie!" he sobbed, his other hand clutching at the edge of the table.

Lanyon didn't know what to do. He could hardly just stand here and watch the wretched man die. At the same time, he didn't trust him: he wasn't going to lower the revolver.

"What do you need?" he said at last. "How can I help you?"

"A beaker!" screamed Hyde. "A moment to mix the compound!"

Still holding the revolver pointed at the visitor, Lanyon reached behind him to take an empty beaker from the shelf.

"Here," he said, putting it down on the table. Hyde grabbed it and, hands trembling feverishly, ripped the cork out of the jar containing the vile-smelling blood-red liquid. Lanyon took a step backward as a plume of white fumes rose, but they didn't seem to affect Hyde, who was already unscrewing the top of one of the bottles of powder.

The little man dribbled some of the liquid into the beaker Lanyon had given him. Even though his whole body was shaking with urgency, he poured carefully, watching the level of the liquid rise against the gradations etched into the beaker's side. Once he was satisfied that he had exactly the right amount, he recorked the jar and put it to one side. Lanyon could see he was having to exert an almost superhuman effort to keep his twitching limbs under control.

"Hastie," said Hyde. "I'll give you one warning. You can go out and close the door and see nothing of what happens next. I'll let myself out the back way, and no one will ever be any the wiser."

Hyde's teeth were clenched and his face was contorting with the effort of forming each tortuous word, but Lanyon could see he was determined to finish his speech.

"Or, if you insist," Hyde hissed, "you can stay in here and witness what happens next. You'll solve a mystery that has been troubling much of London... but it won't bring you much contentment. I cannot be held responsible for the consequences should you stay. I would advise you against it. But it's your own choice."

"I'll stay," said Lanyon, his voice quivering. "I don't trust you out of my sight."

Hyde put his head to one side. "Fair enough," he said. "But you've been warned."

As Lanyon watched, Hyde, working as carefully as before, tapped some of the powder into the beaker of red liquid. He swirled the beaker around, and the liquid turned blue. Again Lanyon sensed that Hyde was having to strain to maintain control of his body; that his limbs wanted to burst into explosive motion, but that his mind was keeping them in check. Hyde added a little more powder and swirled the beaker again; now the liquid was losing its sheen of blue and becoming a muddy brown. The little man grunted in satisfaction.

"A final warning, Hastie," he said. His face was now a truly alarming shade of purple, almost black. He was obviously in excruciating agony. Lanyon was rooted to the spot.

"Can't bear to tear yourself away, eh?" added Hyde with an attempt at a laugh. "Well, be it on your own head."

He gave the beaker one last shake and, before Lanyon could move to stop him, threw his head back and drained the liquid in a single gulp.

Then he shrieked as if his insides were being wrenched out. He clutched his throat and staggered backward, tripping over a stool and crashing to the floor. Lanyon stared in amazement. Hyde's eyes rolled up in their sockets and his head jerked from side to side as if an unseen hand were trying to twist it off his neck. His heels drummed on the thin consulting-room carpet.

How long this went on Lanyon couldn't guess. It could have been half a minute or half an hour. He turned away, unable to watch what he assumed was a ghastly and prolonged death agony. But, when at last the high screeching stopped, he could hear the man's ragged breathing. Then a voice, slightly hoarse but quite calm, as if merely remarking on the weather, said to him: "So now you know my little secret, eh, Hastie?"

Lanyon looked round. "Henry!"

"None other." Jekyll was picking himself up off the floor, moving warily and grimacing as if his joints were hurting him. "Dr. Henry Jekyll, until two years ago a respectable member of the medical profession, and now... this!"

Lanyon sank into the chair. "This is impossible!"

"Not impossible." Jekyll moved to sit down behind the desk, as if he were Dr. Lanyon and Lanyon his patient. "Just improbable."

"But..."

Jekyll held up a hand. "Now you know the truth, Hastie, and yet you know none of it. Let me explain. It's about time I was able to talk to someone about all that I've done. And who better to talk to than an old and dear friend?" He grimaced again. "Although we've had our ups and downs, hmm? Still... still, let me have my say."

Lanyon felt a cold sweat on his brow. He was not a young man, and in recent years his health had not been good. His heart was still pounding violently from the shock of what had happened. And what *had* happened? How had Jekyll substituted himself for the evil-faced man who had been here until moments ago?

Then he looked down at Jekyll's hands and recognized the cuff-links – the same ones Hyde had been wearing when he raised the beaker to his lips – and at last he had some glimmer of understanding.

"Hyde," he croaked. "Jekyll. You're both one and the same man!"

"Yes," said Jekyll sadly. "That's the truth of it."

"But... how?"

A rueful smile appeared on Jekyll's lips.

"A few years ago," he said, "you told me that my theories were insane. Well, you were right – and wrong. You were wrong because my theories were perfectly correct, *dreadfully* correct! You were right because, now, I can see that it was insane to follow

106

them as far as I did. Oh, I have done dreadful things in the name of science, Hastie!"

He put his hands to his face and began to weep.

Lanyon, his chest tight, said: "Tell me everything, Henry."

So, composing himself, Jekyll told him.

"Years ago, when I was still a young man and not long established as a doctor," said Jekyll, "I led a merry life. I had inherited enough money to keep me in comfort for the rest of my days, and I was also earning a fair income from my practice. When the last patient left each evening, I could either stay at home and read or I could go out on the town. What choice would any young man have made?

"So by day I was the sober, steady Dr. Jekyll, trusted by his patients and respected by his peers in the medical profession. And by night – ah, by night I was wild Henry, known in all the music halls and drinking dens of Whitechapel and Soho. My private life was one of wine, women and song. Nothing could have been more unlike the personality I presented to the world during surgery hours!

"The strain of leading this double life eventually became too much for me. I had to abandon either staid Dr. Jekyll or wild Henry, and of course it was my loose-living self that I dropped, throwing all my energies into the pursuit of science and into doing various charitable works, helping the poor where I could, and making gifts of money to several hospitals.

"But I couldn't just *forget* the way I'd been. And you see, Hastie, the whole business began to strike me as most peculiar. During those years I had been, in effect, *two quite different people*. If you'd seen prim Dr. Jekyll in the street, his umbrella neatly furled, beside wild Henry, with a drunken woman on each arm, you wouldn't have thought the two men were related, let alone the same person. I don't even know if the pair of them, if you'd introduced them to one another, would have had anything much to say to each other.

"So I began to ask myself some questions. Now that I was, or so it seemed, entirely Dr. Jekyll, where had wild Henry gone? Had he just been destroyed entirely, this other human being? I couldn't believe it. Or was he still living inside me, biding his time? That seemed altogether more likely. He was the other side of my coin. He was the rascally hell-raiser, while I was the pillar of society. While the pillar of society lived his life out as Dr. Jekyll, the hell-raiser slumbered.

"But I soon came to see that this picture wasn't completely correct. There were bits of wild Henry that showed in the character of Dr. Jekyll, and there had always been bits of Dr. Jekyll evident in wild Henry's personality – for wild Henry had never done anything vicious or spiteful... anything truly *wrong*, even if society might have strongly disapproved of his activities. Wild Henry had even done deeds of kindness, helping people with one hand while lifting a bottle to his lips with the other. So it wasn't a simple case of Jekyll being good and wild Henry being evil.

"Yet there was certainly more good than evil in Jekyll, and certainly more evil than good in wild Henry. They were, like the whole of me, a mixture. Although I appeared to the world at large to be just one person, in fact I was two: an evil person and a good one. It struck me that, if I could isolate the evil person from the good in some way, I might be able to eject the evil person from myself entirely. And I wasn't just thinking of myself.

"*Everyone*, unless they are a perfect saint (and I don't accept there are such paragons any more than you do, Hastie) *everyone*, I say, is made up of these two individuals: a good person and an evil one. How much happier would the world be if it were filled only with good persons! *Then* there might be perfect saints whom you and I could believe in!

"It was at about this time that I began to question the nature of the body. (This was the question I was asking, if you recall, when you broke off our friendship, Hastie. But I had been asking it of myself for years before then.) Our bodies seem to us firm and solid and, except as we age, unchanging. Our souls live in our bodies but, we think, do not affect them in any way. This struck me as implausible. If we come to live in a new house, we soon change it one way or the other, so that it better expresses our own character: Dr. Jekyll, for example, put grey, drab curtains in his windows, but wild Henry, if he had ever been allowed to have his way, would have replaced them with gaudy cloth. Why, then, should the soul be satisfied with the house – the body – in which it lived? Wouldn't it want to... change the curtains, as it were. And the paintwork. And perhaps even build a new bay window?

"In short, the soul would remodel the body in order to express itself more suitably.

"I can see you wanting to object, Hastie, and you are quite right to do so. We've all known beautiful women and handsome men with devils' hearts. But those lovely exteriors are, surely, part of their souls' treachery! And we've known hideous-looking people, ugly people, who are the kindest and finest human beings imaginable. But, in those instances, isn't it the case that their souls are splendid enough not to contain pride, not to need any outward display of prettiness?

"I began to experiment with various chemicals. Of course, I used those drugs only on myself – I knew how dangerous my research was becoming. And I discovered that, yes, I could alter my body. Just a little, and not for very long. If I'd published my results at that stage, Hastie, can you imagine how the scientific world would have hailed me? My name would have gone down in history as the greatest medical theorist of all time!

"But... but even the sober Dr. Jekyll was no saint. I kept the results to myself. Vanity drove me. I wanted to announce something much more spectacular to the world! All this time I had been continuing my parallel experimentation into the possibility of divorcing the evil person inside me from the good, and now it seemed that I would soon be able to bring together the two strands of research.

"It was a lot more difficult than I'd thought it would be. I was so close, and yet it took me several years of cautious, patient experimentation, changing the dosages by the tiniest of fractions here and the merest grain there. But at last, at last I triumphed!

"That was the foulest triumph a man has ever achieved, as I now know.

"I sat down one night – late, after the servants had gone to bed – and I mixed up the precise concoction

I required. I said a prayer, Hastie, if you can believe this, that I would use my knowledge wisely and for the benefit of humanity. I believed I was on the verge of saving the world.

"And then I drank the potion.

"Nothing happened for a minute or two, and I began to think that, in my excitement, I must have measured the ingredients wrongly. But then, all of a sudden, the changes were upon me.

112

"It was agony, Hastie – agony! That first time was the worst, and even the memory of it makes a scream of pain begin to rise in my throat. My teeth ground together as if they were going to wear each other away. The plates of my skull grew and shrank, their edges wrenching and tearing. My jaw seemed about to leap from its sockets. Every joint in my body seemed to be aflame. I really thought I was going to die. I prayed to be *allowed* to die.

"And then, slowly, the pain receded. I began to see the world clearly again – more clearly than I had ever seen it before. My senses were heightened extraordinarily. The air of the dissecting room, which if I'd noticed it at all before I'd have said was stuffy and rank, was now filled with all kinds of delightful scents: even the slight tang of decay from the sink's drain seemed to me to be a delicious, bracing smell. The tiniest sound sang to me. I felt I could have heard a sparrow in a distant, deserted glade… just like God Himself.

"And, most of all, I felt *life*, Hastie. I was a young man again! I could sense the throb of existence in every last cell of my body. My blood was no longer just blood – it was *wine*! The wine that the gods on Olympus drank!

"But what I had never known before was that life was not virtuous. It was not self-sacrificing. It did not believe in the merits of performing charitable works.

"In the terms that you and I – conscious human beings – use, *life was evil!*

"I wallowed in it! I danced in it! I was the wickedest person that ever lived! There wasn't a scrap of goodness in me! I was the master of the world, because I wasn't hampered by even the slightest trace of morality! I could do anything I liked, and already my mind was brimming with evil deeds!

"I grabbed a mirror and took a look at myself. I was smaller than Dr. Jekyll – poor, ineffectual Jekyll, whom I now despised. And I looked half his age. I was also, I persuaded myself, twice as handsome – and, even if I weren't, what did it matter when I had the undiluted power to make sure that everybody thought me so?

"But then I paused. The man I had become was far from lacking in cunning. Lesser creatures the rest of the world might be, but they could still, because of their numbers, overpower and hang me. I couldn't just commit all the acts of gleeful wickedness I wanted to in the full gaze of the world!

"I needed somewhere to hide. In a moment I saw the answer: where better to hide myself than behind

the mask of that respected, boring, hideously dreary pillar of society, Dr. Henry Jekyll?

"I mixed up a beakerful of potion again. It had worked one way. Would it work the other? I drank it down before I could have a chance to think. And it did work! The pains were almost as bad as before, but this time I luxuriated in them. For isn't pain one of the purest expressions of *life* there is? Long moments passed before the sweet agony ebbed away...

"And when I looked in the mirror again, there was Henry Jekyll."

Jekyll stopped speaking.

There was a long silence before Dr. Lanyon coughed. The noise seemed to startle Jekyll out of a trance.

"That was the first time I encountered Edward Hyde," he said. "I called him 'Hyde' because, of course..."

"Yes," said Lanyon. "I understood that. Because he had to hide. Jekyll," he continued, shifting in his seat.

"I think you've told me quite enough – far more than I ever wished to hear. I'd be grateful if you went now; if you left this house and never returned again." Lanyon picked up his spectacles from where they had fallen, unnoticed, into his lap, and settled them back on his nose.

"Do you know 'The Rime of the Ancient Mariner', Hastie?" said Jekyll quietly. "The poem by Coleridge? Once the Ancient Mariner had started to tell his story, there was no way it could be stopped until it was finished. I'm like the Ancient Mariner, Hastie... but my story is a longer one, and far more frightful than his."

And, as Lanyon sat powerless to move, Jekyll proceeded to tell him all the hideous things that Hyde had done.

Back to the Cabinet

Several days later, Lanyon accepted the fact that he was dying. He had not been a well man before that dreadful night when Edward Hyde had come to his house. What Henry Jekyll had told him of Hyde's doings had been so ghastly, so inconceivably vile, that it had sounded his death-knell. His body no longer wished to live, if human life could encompass such loathsomeness. All the police estimates of Hyde's crimes were woefully inadequate: the man had murdered dozens of times. And the things he had done to his victims before they died...

Hastie Lanyon wanted no further part of this world. He looked forward to dying. He didn't care if Heaven awaited him or emptiness: even emptiness would be better than this existence. And anyway, what Jekyll had told him had shaken his faith that there might be a heaven.

But, before he could depart this life, he had certain responsibilities to the living. He had promised Jekyll, before the man had slipped away into the pink-orange light of dawn, that he would never reveal his secret as long as they both should live. He felt that the circumstances were such that he really should break

his promise immediately, but he couldn't bring himself to do so. What he *could* do, however, was to leave an account to be read by others after they had both died.

He summoned his failing energies one evening and wrote everything down. Reliving it was almost as painful as listening to it the first time had been, but he persevered. How much worse must it be, he thought, for Jekyll, knowing not just that these repulsive deeds had been done, but that it was his own flesh and blood, his own other self, that had done them? Hastie Lanyon was not an especially forgiving man, but he forgave Henry Jekyll mostly because of the mental torture he knew the man must be suffering every moment of every day.

For Jekyll had told him one more thing, just before vanishing into the dawn. Just over two months before, he had sworn to himself never to touch the potion again; to let Edward Hyde be dead forever.

And, for nearly eight weeks, his restraint had been enough. Edward Hyde had, apparently, disappeared, and Henry Jekyll was free to live his own life.

But Hyde, like wild Henry before him, had only been sleeping. One night, without any need for the potion, he had broken through again, throwing off Jekyll like someone throwing off an overcoat. It had taken all the efforts of the tiny piece of Jekyll that survived with Hyde to drag the little man back to the Cabinet and force him to mix another dose of potion, and drink it. Since then, at any moment, Hyde could suddenly reappear.

It could happen in the street, when Jekyll was out walking. It might happen at the theatre, if Jekyll were fool enough to go there. It might happen *anywhere*. So Jekyll kept himself locked away in his Cabinet, conserving his energies so that, whenever Hyde thrust himself back into existence, the doctor might force him to drink more potion. But the night before Jekyll had come to Lanyon's house in Cavendish Square, the doctor hadn't been able to restrain his other self. Hyde had gone drinking and carousing all over Whitechapel in a binge that had lasted through the next day. When at last Jekyll had been able to exercise some command over his other self, he had found the police secretly guarding his home. He knew that he couldn't go there without being arrested on sight, so he wrote two letters, one to Lanyon and one to Poole, and gave an urchin a halfpenny to deliver them both.

But Jekyll was uncertain he would be able to bring even this much control to bear another time. And it could be no more than a matter of days, surely, until Hyde battled his way into existence again, perhaps, this time, for good. Especially since, during the two months that Hyde had been banished from the world, the pharmacist who had supplied Jekyll with the drugs he needed for the potion had gone out of business. Other pharmacies supplied what seemed to be exactly the same, but the mixture was not absolutely identical. And the potion made from these drugs didn't work.

Jekyll no longer had the means to banish Hyde.

The envelope was among the rest of the morning's letters, and at first Gabriel Utterson paid it no special attention. It was only when he was about to slit it open that he noticed the envelope was unusually bulky. Inside was a note and another sealed envelope. The note said:

Gabriel,

The enclosed letter is for you, but do not read it yet. I have given my word to Dr. Henry Jekyll — and how I curse the day I ever heard that name! — that what it contains shall not be revealed to the world until he and I are dead.

I have issued instructions to my butler to send this to you after my death, which, as I write, I do not expect to be more than a few days away. I hope and pray that the death of Dr. Henry Jekyll will not be much longer postponed than my own.

Harsh words to use of an old friend? I trust you will understand and share my views when you have read my letter.

Yours,
Hastie Lanyon

Utterson put the sealed envelope away in his safe before he allowed his grief to flood over him; grief over Lanyon's death, and over the way in which, as he thought, scientific rivalry between two of his friends had descended so suddenly into such bitter hatred.

He cried like an infant.

After Lanyon's funeral, held on a bleak day a week later, Utterson hurried home to his dinner. Sleet had tormented the mourners as they stood around the graveside, and steam rose from his damp trouser-legs as he ate. Usually after a funeral Utterson felt his heart lighten, as if his soul recognized that the burial marked some official end to mourning, but this time he remained heavy-spirited. The matter of Jekyll was still nagging away at the back of his mind.

He was startled, though in a way only half-surprised, when Molyneaux interrupted to tell him that Dr. Jekyll's butler, Poole, had called, and was waiting for him in the hall. Utterson put his knife and fork to one side and, still wiping his lips with his napkin, hurried downstairs to meet the elderly servant.

"What's the matter?" he said at once. "What's happened to Jekyll? It must be something serious for him to have sent you out on a vile night like this."

"He didn't send me, Mr. Utterson," said Poole nervously. "I came of my own accord." Now this *did* surprise the lawyer. "But it is about the master," continued Poole. "You see, sir, I'm frightened for him. I'm frightened *of* him, as well. We all are – all us servants. We've taken as much as we can, and then a bit more, and now we've just had enough. So, as you're the only friend the master has left, I thought I should come to you."

Utterson groaned. "Tell me what's wrong this time, Poole."

"He's locked himself away in his Cabinet these past eight days, and he won't come out for all our pleadings. We leave food outside on a tray by the door, and sometimes it's taken though most often it's not, but we never see him. And sometimes the voice that shouts back at us doesn't sound like his voice at all, but like the other gentleman's. And once or twice I swear I've heard them both in there, arguing as if the whole world's at stake. And sometimes..."

"Enough," said Utterson, raising a palm to stem the flow of words. "Can't you see what's going on through the window?"

"He's put a cloth over it," replied Poole, his hands twitching anxiously. "We can't see anything. All we can do is hear, and that's bad enough."

"It might just be a difficult experiment," began Utterson.

"That's what we thought at first. He's had us scouring all the chemists in London for some compound he needs – we must have brought it to him a hundred times or more. But each time it seems it isn't good enough. For minutes after it's gone from where we leave it outside the door, we hear him moaning and yelling, as if Satan himself were teasing his soul. We're at our wits' end!"

Looking into Poole's eyes, Utterson believed it. "I'd better come to the house," he said.

Poole's face lit up. "Would you, sir?" he said. "We were hoping you would say that. Perhaps he might come out for you, his dearest friend, where he's ignored all our appeals."

"Let's hope so," said Utterson glumly. But in his heart he wasn't optimistic. He sensed that the end of the strange story of Dr. Henry Jekyll was in sight.

"Molyneaux!" he called. "My coat!"

It was a wild night. A pale moon lay on her back as though the wind had tilted her. The wind made talking difficult, and seemed to have swept the streets bare of pedestrians, for Utterson thought he had never seen this part of London so deserted. He wished it weren't so, for he felt a desperate need for the presence of other human beings; his mind was full of a crushing presentiment of calamity.

When he and Poole reached the door of Jekyll's house, they paused a moment, as if to gather strengh for what they might find inside. Across the street, the howling wind was forcing the thin trees of the garden in the middle of the square to lash themselves against the railings. It was not a reassuring sight.

"Here goes, then," said Utterson dourly.

"Here goes, indeed," said Poole. "May God be with us."

"Amen."

The other servants had chained the door, and opened it only when Poole shouted his name through the letterbox. Inside, Utterson found all of Jekyll's staff huddled together. When they saw him, a housemaid began to weep shrilly, and the cook came running forward as if to take him in her arms.

"Stop this at once!" the laywer snapped. "What would your master say if he could see you like this?"

"You must forgive them, sir" said Poole quietly. "They're terrified." Then, not aware of any contradiction, he bellowed at the housemaid to shut up, threatening to fire her that very night if she didn't control herself.

"Let's get this over with as quickly as possible," said Utterson when the butler had calmed down. It was obvious to him that Poole was not far short of cracking. *And you could say the same about me*, thought Utterson grimly.

The two men, with some of the servants trailing behind them, went through the house and across the back yard to the dissecting room door. In the enclosed space of the yard the wind seemed like a living thing, dancing and capering and pulling at the men's coats. Utterson looked up and saw thin, shredded clouds chasing each other across the crooked smile of the moon.

"Let's get this over with," he said again. "Knock at the door, man."

Poole obeyed.

The door of the dissecting room swung open. Inside was blackness. Poole, clearly terrified, would have fallen down the steps if Utterson had not caught his arm to steady him.

"It's the first time in over a week it's been unlocked," whispered the butler. "He had a brand-new lock fitted after Dr. Lanyon was here, and he kept the only key." He hesitated, then added: "I... I dread to go in there, sir."

Utterson found himself stuttering with fear. "T-t-to tell you the truth," he said, "so do I."

"But we must," said Poole. Gesturing to the others to keep their distance, he held out a candle. The lawyer cupped his hands around the wick, and Poole lit it. Then the two men advanced, step by trembling step, into the dissecting room.

As soon as they were inside, a blanket of silence descended on them. It was as if the windswept night outside were a hundred miles away. The dim light of the candle seemed pitifully weak. The surgical theatre seemed huge, and somehow its shadows seemed all the wrong shape.

Poole lifted the candle high above him. Utterson could make out the laboratory bench, cluttered with equipment. Boxes and papers lay everywhere on the floor. In the corner he could see the bulk of the electricity-generating machine: to his seething mind it looked as it were crouching, waiting to pounce on the intruders.

"I can't see him," he said at last. His voice sounded hoarse, and he cleared his throat self-consciously. "Can you?"

Before Poole could answer there was a low moan, and both men started.

"What was that?" whispered Utterson.

Poole swallowed loudly. "It came from the Cabinet, sir," he said. "I think." He nodded towards the steps and the door at the far end of the theatre. "In there."

Picking their way with difficulty through the darkness across the littered floor, the men crept to the foot of the Cabinet's steps. They shrugged at each other. What next?

"It's my duty, sir," whispered Poole. He climbed the steps reluctantly, clearly ready to bolt at any instant, and quietly knocked.

Once. Twice.

Again that moan from within, then a low voice. "Go away."

"It's Mr. Utterson here to see you," said Poole loudly. "Mr. Utterson the lawyer."

"Tell him to go away as well," shouted the voice. "I cannot see anyone." And then it began to sob.

Poole tugged the lawyer away from the door to the far side of the theatre. Through the open door to the yard, Utterson could see the servants' anxious faces, but again there was that feeling that they were a great distance away.

"Tell me," demanded Poole urgently, "was that my master's voice?"

"It seemed... very much changed," answered Utterson slowly. He felt his face grow pale.

"*Changed!*" said Poole, with a snort. "I've been twenty years in my master's service. Do you think I wouldn't know his voice? Sir, that was not him!"

"Then who was it?" hissed Utterson, though in his heart of hearts he knew the answer. Even so, he tried to find some other explanation. "Perhaps he's suffering from one of those terrible diseases that punish the body so dreadfully that the voice is changed entirely. No wonder he sends you and the others out to scour the local pharmacies for the drug he needs to cure himself! He recognizes his own illness, and seeks to..."

"That was not his voice," said Poole, flatly.

"Then," said Utterson after a long pause, "then we must find out whose voice it was. We must break down the door."

"There's a fire-axe on the wall, sir," said Poole. He turned to the servants outside. "One of you go and fetch the poker from the kitchen for Mr. Utterson," he called.

Utterson should have felt more confident with the heavy poker in his hand, but he didn't. He was aware of Poole instructing a footman to go around to the door in Mitre Court and guard it, but his thoughts were elsewhere. Behind the Cabinet's red door, he was certain, he and Poole would find Henry Jekyll, but whether the doctor was dead or alive was something he couldn't guess. And what of the other voice that had replied to them? The voice that Poole insisted was not his master's was one that Utterson was certain he recognized from another cold night, long ago, when he had laid his hand on the shoulder of a little man at the dissecting room's rear door.

"Hyde," he breathed.

Poole heard him. "I think so too, sir," he said.

The two men stood looking at each other. "I've sent the knife-boy to fetch the police, but I think my master would prefer it if we were the ones who..."

His voice trailed away, but Utterson knew what the butler was thinking. A police siege would be splashed all over the newspapers tomorrow and Jekyll would not wish it. Better, even if they found the man dead, not to let his name be dragged through the gutter like that.

"I agree," he said. "I wish I didn't."

Poole fetched the fire-axe from its hook on the wall. The two men once again stole across the floor to the base of the steps leading up to the Cabinet.

Utterson touched Poole's arm, and nodded to the man to keep silent.

"Jekyll!" he shouted. "It's me! Utterson! I demand to see you at once!"

"Go away!" shrieked the voice from behind the door.

Hyde's voice. The lawyer was sure of it now, but he tried one last time.

"I warn you, Jekyll, that if you do not open this door we will break it down! Let us in!" He took the candle from the butler's shaking hand.

"Utterson!" cried the voice. "For God's sake have mercy."

The lawyer could bear it no longer. "That's Hyde," he shouted. "Smash the lock, Poole! Hurry!"

The butler swung the axe. The crash sounded like thunder in the dissecting room. The door jumped on its hinges. Wood splintered. From beyond the door there was a piercing scream of raw animal terror.

"Again!" yelled Utterson.

Another crash. Another scream. The door held. Poole cursed.

"Again!" bellowed the lawyer. The head of the axe caught in the wood of the door, just above the lock, and Poole tugged to work it free.

"No! No! No!" came Hyde's voice.

And then there was a dreadful silence except for Poole's gasps and the squeak as the axe pulled clear.

"Wait," said Utterson. He didn't know why.

They stayed motionless, both of them breathing heavily. From the other side of the door there was a terrible, strained, agonized sigh and the noise of something heavy falling to the floor.

Utterson found there were tears in his eyes. "I think it's over," he said quietly. "One more blow of your axe should let us in, Poole."

"I don't like to think of what we shall find, sir," said the butler, hefting the axe uneasily as if reluctant to use it.

"Nevertheless," said Utterson, "we must go in."

"We must," agreed Poole, and once again he swung the axe.

The lock broke and the door fell askew. Jumping ahead of the butler, Utterson pushed it open with his shoulder.

At first glance there seemed nothing wrong. A fire was burning in the hearth, and tables and chairs were placed neatly around. Two of the drawers of the desk were open and some papers had fallen to the floor, as if someone had been searching through them, hopelessly, time after time, hunting for something that wasn't there – but otherwise, apart from a picture hanging crooked on the wall, the room was as tidy as if it had been prepared for a tea party.

Except for the body that lay face down and horribly twisted in the middle of the floor.

Utterson, with Poole at his shoulder, ran to it. As he knelt down beside the body, the limbs gave one final convulsion and were still. Utterson clutched at the wrist, trying to feel a pulse, but there was nothing.

"Dead," he said bitterly.

"Yes, sir," said Poole, seemingly calm again now that the worst had been revealed. "But *who's* dead?"

Jekyll's Last Letter

Utterson never forgot what happened next. Still kneeling, he looked up at Poole, then looked down again. *I don't want to do this!* his mind screamed at him. Ignoring it, he reached out and gently rolled the body over.

The face staring glassily towards the ceiling was contorted as if in fear of the very Devil himself. There was purple froth around its lips, and the eyes seemed almost to have leaped from their sockets.

But it was unmistakably the face of Edward Hyde. *Then where was Henry Jekyll?*

Much, much later Gabriel Utterson sat behind his desk in his own office, looking in horror at the three letters that lay in front of him. The first was very short. Poole had found it on the doctor's desk, and wordlessly passed it to the lawyer. It read:

My dear Gabriel,

When you have this in your hands, I will have disappeared — in one way or another. I do not know exactly what is going to happen to me, but all my instincts tell me

that the end is sure and that it cannot be far away. Although my body may, in terribly different form, still walk this earth, you may be certain, Gabriel, that your old and undeserving friend Henry Jekyll will be dead.

Hastie Lanyon told me he had sent you a letter detailing all that happened between him and myself the other night. Read it, and then read the narrative you will find in the bottom left-hand drawer of my desk in the Cabinet. I fear I am asking you to do a lot of reading, dear friend! Yet I hope you will come to understand that this sorry individual is no demon wallowing in wickedness, but instead a man who, though blinded perhaps by vanity, sought only to bring benefit to the world. That it should have come to this is, I believe you will agree, a matter for all of our griefs.

But you yourself must judge your most respectful and admiring of acquaintances,

Henry Jekyll

Utterson turned over the two other documents on the desk yet again. He had read both of them twice, and had no wish to do so again. The whole terrible truth about Dr. Jekyll and Mr. Hyde was set out in them. Of how the doctor, seeking glory where he could have sought only knowledge, had kept everything to himself until it was too catastrophically late. And of how he had become addicted to the *life* he gained whenever he walked the world in the guise of Hyde – the other person, the one made up from the evil that dwelled within Jekyll. Yes, Jekyll had become *addicted*, there was no other word for it, to the sense of freedom he had when he threw off the shackles of responsiblity towards others and allowed himself to do exactly what he wanted.

Utterson mused sadly. The trouble was that no one could do exactly what they wanted, and only a fool would try. People had to live with each other. They had to discover the much greater pleasures that came from helping one another. Sir Danvers Carew had had it right: he had devoted much of himself to improving the lives of the poor, and even as he died on that cold pavement down by the river, with the cruel blows of Hyde's heavy stick raining down on his head, he must have known the true happiness of having spent his life well.

The lawyer looked back over his own actions of the past months, and found much to criticize. He had been too much concerned with public appearances, too little with the good of his fellow human beings. He should have told the police at once of the connection between Dr. Jekyll and Mr. Hyde, not held back hoping that the whole affair could be swept under the carpet and forgotten about; had he done so, perhaps Jekyll and several murdered innocents would still be alive. Their lost lives were, in part, Utterson's own fault. Evils didn't just go away because you wanted them to. You had to work to get rid of them.

For Jekyll, he was surprised to discover, he felt nothing at all – no compassion, no grief, not even any hatred. Just nothing. For a time he had thought that Jekyll was a good man lured into wickedness by circumstances. Then he had thought him a fool.

But Jekyll could have stopped everything before it had properly begun. He could have asked his friends for help. Instead, fascinated by his creation, he had played with it, heedless of the consequences, until it had become too great for him. Until *it* was playing with *him*.

It wasn't just the body of Edward Hyde – or Henry Jekyll – that had died last night, Utterson realized, but Jekyll himself and everything that Utterson had ever liked or admired about him. For the man was dead in Utterson's heart.

Grunting at the pains in his stiff old joints, the lawyer heaved himself to his feet. He picked up the three letters, glanced at them one last time, then very deliberately fed them to the fire. It took some time before the last of the pages crumbled to ash, but Utterson was patient.

Then, dusting his hands, he went upstairs to bed.

Novels and Movies about Jekyll and Hyde

The book you have just read is a complete retelling of Robert Louis Stevenson's original story. To make the story easier to read, there have been a few minor changes, though these do not affect the overall plot. This is not the first time another writer has sought a new approach to the story or investigated similar themes. Several novels and movies have put their own interpretations on the story. Here are some of them.

Novels and stories

The Picture of Dorian Gray (1891) by Oscar Wilde, tells a story different from Stevenson's, but the basic idea is rather similar. Dorian Gray is a man who stays looking youthful and innocent while leading a life of excess and cruelty. But many people are taken in by his good looks and charm because he never appears to grow any older and remains physically unaffected by his lifestyle. Instead, all these changes appear on a portrait of him painted years before, which he keeps locked away. When people finally discover the portrait, they realize that the smiling face of Dorian Gray in fact conceals a despicably evil man.

The Man who Saw the Devil (1934), by James Corbett, returns to Stevenson's idea of one man living a double life, but in this case neither of the two personalities knows about the existence of the other.

Methinks the Lady (1945), by S. Guy Endore, concerns a woman who has Jekyll-and-Hyde characteristics. It gives a psychoanalytical explanation for this sort of situation, looking at the mind of the victim and what causes her actions.

The Dark Other (1950), by the U.S. science-fiction writer Stanley G. Weinbau, once again explores the situation in terms of people's understanding of psychology in the 1940s.

In *The Trial of John and Henry Norton* (1973), by Roland Puccetti, surgeons cut the link between the two lobes of a man's brain, and each lobe becomes in effect a separate person. One of the Nortons commits murder but, because the two share the same body, they have to be tried together.

Dr. Jekyll and Mr. Holmes (1979), by Loren D. Estleman, features Sherlock Holmes investigating the case of Dr. Jekyll.

Jekyll, Alias Hyde (1988), by Donald Thomas, is a detective story. Inspector Swain and Sergeant Lumley pursue the killer of Sir Danvers Carew and in the end find a perfectly rational explanation for how two men might seem to share a single body.

Two Women of London: The Strange Case of Ms. Jekyll and Mrs. Hyde (1989), by Emma Tennant, is a feminized version of the story.

The Jekyll Legacy (1990), by Robert Bloch and Andre Norton, is a continuation of Stevenson's story.

Mary Reilly (1990), by Valerie Martin, tells the whole story from the point of view of a maid working in Dr. Jekyll's house, and coming to love him.

If you want to find out more about all these different retellings of the story, you could try *The Definitive Dr. Jekyll and Mr. Hyde Companion* (1983), by H.M. Geduld.

Movies

The earliest surviving movie of the story was made in 1910 by the Danish director August Blom, though some film historians claim that there was an earlier film, made in America in 1908, which is now lost. The first really successful version was made in 1920 and starred John Barrymore as both Jekyll and Hyde: some critics say this silent film, with its special effects and fine acting, is the best film version of the story. Another lost version is *Der Januskopf* (1920) by the German director F.W. Murnau, who made the great Dracula movie *Nosferatu*.

However, the version usually regarded as the classic is *Dr. Jekyll and Mr. Hyde,* released in 1931. Directed by Rouben Mamoulian, it stars Fredric March (in an award–winning performance) as the two characters. It is available on video and is still sometimes shown on television even today.

Another movie of the story was made in 1941, again called *Dr. Jekyll and Mr. Hyde*, and directed by Victor Fleming. This had a star-filled cast, including Spencer Tracy, Ingrid Bergman and Lana Turner, but it was not a great success. After this, more and more film-makers began to deviate from the original plot, using the names Jekyll and Hyde more as a shorthand for a horror plot about a villain with a hidden life than as a reference to Stevenson's book. Further spin-offs included *Son of Dr. Jekyll* (1951) and *Daughter of Dr. Jekyll* (1957). In 1960 the Hammer studio released *The Two Faces of Dr. Jekyll* (also called *House of Fright* and *Jekyll's Inferno*). Directed by Terence Fisher and starring Christopher Lee and David Kossoff, it is probably the first modern horror film to use the story – though again, much changed from Stevenson's original.

The story was also the source of a number of film comedies. One of the earliest is the Tom and Jerry cartoon *Dr. Jekyll and Mr. Mouse* (1948), which was nominated for an Oscar. *Abbott and Costello Meet Dr. Jekyll and Mr. Hyde* (1954) takes the comedy duo to London, where they hunt down the "monster", who is played by Boris Karloff. *The Nutty Professor* (1963) updates the story to set it on a U.S. university campus. Jerry Lewis plays both Professor Kelp and Buddy Love – the Jekyll and Hyde figures.

Another movie version of the original story appeared in 1968, followed in 1971 by a slightly gory version called *I, Monster*. Strangely, in this later movie, some of the characters' names were changed: Dr. Jekyll becomes Dr. Marlowe and Edward Hyde becomes Edward Blake (both roles are played by Christopher Lee); yet Utterson, Lanyon and the young Richard Enfield appear under their own names.

Dr. Jekyll and Sister Hyde (1971) has the additional twist that Jekyll, on swallowing the potion, turns not into another man but into an evil woman. The two starring actors, Ralph Bates and Martine Beswick, look just like male and female counterparts of a single person, without looking exactly the same.

A French version of the story, *The Strange Case of Dr. Jekyll and Miss Osbourne* (1981), starts with a girl being murdered when she arrives at Dr. Jekyll's house, and proceeds from there. This film has been released under a number of different titles, including *Bloodbath of Dr. Jekyll* and *The Blood of Dr. Jekyll*.

Jekyll and Hyde – Together Again (1982) updates the story, setting it in a modern U.S. hospital. Like *The Nutty Professor,* this is a comedy.

More traditional are *The Jekyll Experiment* (1983) and *Dr. Jekyll and Mr. Hyde* (1986), the latter an Australian animated movie made for television. *Edge of Sanity* (1988), a French movie starring Anthony Perkins (star of Hitchcock's *Psycho*), mixes up Jekyll, Hyde and Jack the Ripper. It's a scary film, but again the plot is rather different from the original. *Mary Reilly* (1995) is a film version of the book by Valerie Martin (see page 140). A remake of *The Nutty*

Professor (1996), based on Jerry Lewis's original screenplay and starring Eddie Murphy, was followed by a sequel, *The Nutty Professor II*, in 2000.

Another Usborne Classic

FRANKENSTEIN
FROM THE STORY BY MARY SHELLEY

He made his way to the tank and peeped over the rim. There was only the smooth, undisturbed surface of the liquid... Confused thoughts and troubled emotions ran through his mind. He had failed, it was true, but maybe that was for the best. He sighed and relaxed slightly. Then, from the liquid, a huge hand shot out to grab him.

As lightning flashes across the night sky, Victor Frankenstein succeeds in the ultimate scientific experiment – the creation of life. But the being he creates, though intelligent and sensitive, is so huge and hideous that it is rejected by its creator, and by everyone else who meets it. Soon, the lonely, miserable monster turns on Victor and his family, with terrifying and tragic results.